FAIR IS FAIR

FAIR IS FAIR

WORLD FOLKTALES OF JUSTICE

SHARON CREEDEN

AUGUST HOUSE PUBLISHERS

ATLANTA

www.augusthouse.com

Printed in the United States of America

10 9 8 7 6 5 4 3 2 1   HB
10 9 8 7 6 5 4 3 2   PB
First Paperback Edition, 1997

LIBRARY OF CONGRESS CATALOGING-IN-PUBLICATION DATA

Creeden, Sharon, 1938—
Fair is fair : world folktales of justice / by Sharon Creeden.
p. cm.
Includes bibliographical references.
ISBN 0-87483-400-7 (alk. paper) ISBN 0-87483-477-5
1. Justice—Folklore. 2. Tales. I. Title.
GR877.C74   1994   94-23850
398'.355—dc20   CIP

President and publisher: Ted Parkhurst
Executive editor: Liz Parkhurst
Project editors: Rufus Griscom, Suzi Parker
Cover illustration: Byron Taylor

AUGUST HOUSE, INC.   PUBLISHERS   ATLANTA

To my husband, Will,
who always supports and
encourages my dreams

CONTENTS

FOREWORD

I once had a book which had on its cover a picture of a boy reading the very same book. On the cover of that small book was, of course, that same boy reading that same book, which in turn had a picture of a boy reading the book on its cover. So it went, on and on. How I have tried to go back through those storybooks within storybooks. That was so very long ago, and I had all but forgotten that book with its magical cover, when I picked up this collection of *World Folktales of Justice*. Here in words was the same magic that my childhood book created in pictures. Here is a book of stories. But when you look and listen more closely, you find that it is really a book of stories within stories within stories within stories.

You look once, and you see simple folktales. Yet these tales are so beautifully crafted that, as you read, you find your lips moving, wanting to read them aloud as they were intended to be read. Then you are swept into the stories themselves, delighting in the wisdom and cleverness of the judges—from Solomon himself to lesser known but equally wise figures such as Judge Coyote of Native American lore, and the magistrate in the tale "Stolen Smells"—and in the often unexpected but always satisfying ways that the rascals and worse get their comeuppance. These are, after all, tales about justice. In these tales the wicked do not prosper, though the crafty do occasionally outwit the self-interested. As W.C. Fields, the comic film star of the decades before World War II, once said, "You can't cheat an honest man," and thus those who attempt to trade goods for money trees, bushes that grow golden pears, and other things that we know we have no right to expect in this life, find themselves worse off than the scoundrel who did the trading. This too is very satisfying; it affirms our sense of fairness.

But if you look again, you will see another story. Ahead of you awaits a remarkable collection of justice tales from an incredible range of cultures, sources, and eras. Look at the table of contents: there are stories from Burma, Denmark, Mexico, Morocco, China, and Japan, to name a few. There are stories from biblical times, medieval days, and the colonial era. Now look at the notes at the end of each tale, which detail the varied sources in which the same tale appears. More than a collection of folktales, this is a work of scholarship that is telling a larger story about these stories. When you see that many of these tales (with minor variation) have been told in widely varied cultures for centuries, you will realize that before you are powerful, enduring conceptions of what is just.

Now look again, and you will see comments following the tales, each telling its own story. This section is a grab bag. Just reach in, take your chances, and see what prize you'll pull out. Sometimes, you will find a story about how the topic in the tale deals with an area of consequence in our own legal system, such as juvenile justice, custody disputes, women's rights, or cruelty to animals. Sometimes it will be about some legal principle buried within the story, like *corpus delicti* or causation. Other times, it will be a tale about the connection between the story and some phenomena in our own culture, such as serial killers or our fascination with outlaws. Or it will be about something of historical interest, such as the Salem Witch Trials or trial by ordeal. When the stories deal with subjects like the death penalty and the insanity defense, however, they offer a greater lesson: even though we all want justice, it is not always easy to figure out what that is.

Look yet again. All I have already discussed is only the beginning, for this collection of tales is not only a celebration of the universal notion of justice; taken collectively, these tales describe the very process by which we actually achieve justice in our own legal system. Here again, we have stories within stories.

To begin, in most of these stories, the characters recount anecdotes, whether they be about their differing understanding of what it means to use a fire ("The Warmth of a Fire"), who owns the smells in the air ("The Stolen Smells"), or what happened to the gold in the olive jar ("Ali Cogia, Merchant of Baghdad"). This, of course, is exactly what happens in a trial. One attorney will tell the jury: Sally Bist was happy, as happy as she had ever been, when she went for a walk that early February morning. She had gotten engaged the night before to the man she had told her friends was "the kindest, most caring person I have ever known." And she had a wonderful job at Ames Tectronix. It was all so perfect. And then she stepped into the crosswalk at Pearl and Elm and everything was taken away from her in the squeal of a cherry-red Porsche convertible driven by the defendant....

The story will then be played out through the attorney's direct-examination of the key eyewitness:

ATTORNEY:	What did you see then?
WITNESS:	She started towards the crosswalk.
ATTORNEY:	How far away were you from her?
WITNESS:	Maybe eight to ten feet.
ATTORNEY:	What was she doing?
WITNESS:	Just walking. Then she looked up and down the street.
ATTORNEY:	And then?
WITNESS:	She stepped into the crosswalk.
ATTORNEY:	And then?
WITNESS:	At that time I heard this loud sound.
ATTORNEY:	Could you describe it?
WITNESS:	An automobile engine roaring, and tires squealing.
ATTORNEY:	And after you heard this sound?
WITNESS:	Suddenly this shiny red Porsche came…

The opposing attorney will then tell a different story. Her eyes were so filled with stars and her mind with wedding bells that she was oblivious to her surroundings and stepped off the curb as the defendant was driving through the crosswalk, making it impossible for him to stop ("…though he tried everything he could do to avoid her, Oh God, how he tried"). The key eyewitness will also be cast in a different light. He was on his way home from the local tavern; he'd always hated the defendant; and so on.

In the tales, the judge must then decide between these competing stories. In many of the stories (such as "Solomon's Judgment," "Ooka and the Wasted Wisdom," and "Ali Cogia") the judge must decide who is telling the truth, but in other tales (like "The Otters and the Fox," "Why Owl Comes Out at Night," and "The Quality of Mercy") the facts are established but their interpretation is disputed. Again, this is precisely the position of a judge or jury in our legal system.

In a much publicized recent case, the legality of a search that produced a bloody article of clothing turned on which story characterization of the events one accepted. Did police vault over the walls surrounding the defendant's home without a warrant because they were fearful for the occupants' safety, or because they wanted to search for evidence? If one accepts the first story version (which the judge did), then the police action is legal. Accept the second story version, and the police action is illegal, and the bloody evidence inadmissable. At this point, one might ask what prevents a judge who is making this type of decision from manipulating the law to reach the ends he or she desires? That is a question that has perplexed past and current legal scholars. The best answer they have been able to come up with is the very one contained in a tale from Africa called "Whose Children?" that appears on the surface to be a children's story. The conclusion of this story as well as the legal scholars is that legal concepts can be manipulated, but our shared sense of what is "just" acts as a practical limit on most judges. Of course, if a judge is driven by bias, self-interest, or fear (as are the animals in the story), the judge cannot be counted on for a fair decision. A neutral, detached judge or jury is foundational to our notion of fair decision making.

That, however, does not end our discussion of the role stories play in achieving justice. The judges in the stories weigh the significance and accuracy of competing accounts by comparing them to their own repertoire of stories about how people behave and should behave. Solomon appears to base his decision on a cultural assumption—a narrative of sorts—that a real mother would rather lose her child to someone else than see it sacrificed. Now one may question whether this underlying cultural assumption or story is accurate. Might not the biological mother think, "I'd rather my child die than live apart from me," or, "she's better off dead than living her life with that beast-woman"? But the point is that the underlying cultural story about the true nature of mothers resolves Solomon's dilemma (even if his true motive was to disclose the best parent rather than the biological mother). Similarly, Judge Coyote resolves the dispute between Rabbit and Snake by referring to his own set of stories about the behavior of snakes and rabbits.

This is precisely how jurors make decisions. In their ground-breaking work, *Reconstructing Reality in the Courtroom*, Lance Bennett and Martha Feldman conducted what is probably the most systematic study ever done of why and how jurors make the decisions they do. They found that jurors place the scattered information presented at trial into narratives. The jurors then compare these presented narratives with the stories they construct privately (constructed from experience, logic, bias, myth, social convention, etc.) about how the situation described in the trial should have taken place. For example, Battered-woman Syndrome testimony (in which an expert describes to the jurors common psychological responses to physical abuse) is really a way of providing the jurors with another story to add to their existing collection of private stories. If we are told that someone is violently beating another person in his or her home, we imagine a story in which this second person (if he or she cannot fight back) leaves, calls for the police, goes to a doctor or to the hospital, etc. If a person does none of these things that beaten people do in our private stories, we likely conclude that he or she is not telling the truth about being beaten. Battered-woman Syndrome testimony tells us that there's another story that is often closer to the truth, a story in which the person beaten does none of the things we expect based upon our preconceived stories.

In fact, the stories in this collection are *themselves* the type of archetypal tales that we carry in our heads when attempting to resolve disputes. Thus, "The Fisherman and the King's Chamberlain" is an expression of the basic principle that being a partner with someone means that you share the bad as well as the good. "Why Owl Comes Out at Night" asserts that if you agree to act as surety for someone (for example, co-sign on his or her car loan), you have made a binding commitment. If that person messes up, you pay; that's what it means to be a surety. "The Stoning" expresses the belief that acknowledgment of guilt is the first step to rehabilitation, and mitigates the punishment one would otherwise merit.

More than underlying the process of resolving individual decisions, stories underlie the very construction of the law. Not so long ago, the cultural story concerning division of labor in American families expressed throughout the law was that women were the childbearers and managed the home, men were the sole wage earners and managed a career, and all families required both a mommy and daddy. In the context of these stories (which, by the way, did not reflect reality even then), a woman's claim of workplace discrimination was not likely to succeed in a court of law. Only when the "story" of the American family changed did the law follow.

All tales come to an ending, and this foreword, a tale about tales about tales, must end as well. This is still the beginning of the book, of course, but the final point I would like to make is about its needed a story; Sandra Ogden, the children's librarian at the King County Library in Burien, Washington, who enthusiastically shared her wisdom and her books; and my great-aunt Evelyn Jones, who was a children's librarian in Wichita, Kansas, and helped me through college.

And I am grateful to my editors at August House: Ted and Liz Parkhurst, who love folktales and dream big dreams, and Rufus Griscom, who has a commitment to excellence and the knack for choosing the right word.

Great is Justice!
Justice is not settled by legislators and
laws—it is in the Soul,
It cannot be varied by statutes, any more
than love, pride, the attraction of gravity can,
It is immutable—it does not depend on
majorities—majorities or what not
come at last before the same
passionless and exact tribunal.

—WALT WHITMAN
"Great Are the Myths," in *Leaves of Grass*, 1860.

INTRODUCTION

At age thirty-nine, I went to law school and, after graduating, worked as a deputy prosecuting attorney in King County, Washington. I quickly burned out on the heavy work load. At the same time, I joined the Seattle Storytelling Guild. At first, I thought I was merely improving my speaking and trial skills. But I soon realized that I wanted to tell stories more than I wanted to try cases. Since 1982, my business card has read Storyteller. I tell stories in schools, colleges, parks, and festivals. It is my greatest pleasure to tell tales of justice which link my seemingly disparate careers: law and storytelling.

Our society is eager to hear and read about legal matters these days. Trials are televised live. Television movies recount the latest cases. But even more, people are hungry for fairness. After the acquittal of the police in the Rodney King trial, the shouts from the street were, "No justice, no peace." Indeed, the rallying cry for justice has been sounded throughout world history. And it has been recorded, among other places, in the annals of world folklore. With this book, I offer the folklore wisdom of others who have searched for justice.

In selecting material, I looked for stories that are easily spoken and easily remembered, that through vivid characters and events would delight listeners. These are stories meant to be told aloud, stories smoothed and honed over centuries of telling and retelling. They come from generations of oral tradition. I hope they are just resting lightly on these pages before they come alive through the words of other storytellers, attorneys, teachers, and parents.

Some of the stories reminded me of actual cases, so I have included some legal comments. These comments are meant to show the parallels between ancient folktales and modern legal issues. I hope the comments will stimulate thinking and discussion. The comments vary in length and content and follow most, but not all, of the tales. Some stories prompted a specific criminal case, like "Mr. Fox," which brought to mind Ted Bundy; others lead to general discussions, like "The Quality of Mercy," which raised issues about women and the law.

Although many of these stories deal with judges and court decisions, this is not a book about laws. In the United States, laws are made by elected bodies on every level: by Congress, the legislators of each state, city councils, and county councils. In addition, there are interpretations of these laws made by judges in the cases that come before them. Laws change from state to state, from year to year, from case to case to meet circumstances and shifts in opinions. It is precisely this changing, complex nature that caused me to decide against making this book about law.

Instead, I have selected stories that say something about justice, because, behind—or perhaps above—all laws is the ideal of justice. Justice is enduring and does not alter with a new administration or political whim. Although everyone is confused about the law, no one is confused about justice. The hunger for justice and the recognition of justice is in every heart. Every small child cries, "Hey, that's not fair!"

I have not defined justice in this book; rather, I have let the stories, in total, define justice. And it is left to the reader's heart to respond to each story—either, "Hey, that's not fair!" or "Fair is fair."

⊷ *One* ⊷

WHEN MERCY SEASONS JUSTICE

These stories are about the kind of judges we would wish for if we were going into court. Author Robert Traver described these judges in his novel, *Anatomy of a Murder:*

> Judges, like people, may be divided roughly into four classes: judges with neither head nor heart—they are to be avoided at all costs; judges with head but no heart—they are almost as bad; then judges with heart but no head—risky but better than the first two; and finally, those rare judges who possess both head and a heart—thanks to blind luck, that's our judge.

Judges need a head because they are the "Triers of Facts." They must examine all the evidence and decide what happened. There is usually a conflict about the facts—someone is lying, some facts are missing. Several stories in this section deal with determining the truth; the judges in the Solomon biblical story, the Ooka folktale, and "Ali Cogia, Merchant of Baghdad" are trying to find out the truth.

Sometimes the facts are undisputed, and then it is the duty of the judges to use their hearts to reach the right result. The king in "The Pear Seed" provides a good example of how to let the wisdom of the heart guide decisions. The magistrate in "The Stolen Smells" uses his humor (and there is wisdom in humor) to reach a fair result.

Two of the judges are wise enough to listen to advice; King David listens to his son Solomon in "The Warmth of a Fire," and the king listens to his daughter, disguised as a lawyer, in "The Quality of Mercy." Using the wisdom of their children, these judges avoided the unfair results of enforcing technicalities or the "letter of the law."

The judges in the stories that follow have been the custodians of justice for centuries; they are themselves the "spirit of the law."

The Stolen Smells

🙰

(United States)

Once upon a time, there was a baker who owned a shop in a small town. This baker was a stingy man, stingy with his greetings and smiles. In his shop, he never put out a small dish of samples or gave a cookie to a child.

But he was a skilled baker; his cinnamon buns and his breads were finely made. The people of the town flocked to buy them. They were drawn into his shop by the sweet smells wafting into the street. The baker liked to watch the shoppers strolling down the avenue. One by one they sniffed and smiled and came into his shop.

But not everyone who smelled his delicious smells came inside and made a purchase. Some merely stood outside, smelling and peering into the windows. The baker thought, "They are filling their bellies on the scent of my bread. And here I am without a penny for all my hard work." If only he could have bottled and corked up those delicious smells, he would have placed them on the shelf to be bought and sold like bread.

One winter morning, just after dawn, the baker was in his shop baking bread. He kneaded and twisted the dough in a big wooden trough. He did not sing while he worked. Instead, he muttered and complained about the price of flour and the cost of firewood.

He looked up and saw someone peering in the window. It was a man in a shabby coat. The man gazed at a row of warm raisin bread, and he hungrily breathed in great chunks of the fragrant air. The very sight of him angered the baker. "There's a thief, stealing my smells, filling his belly, and not a penny for me."

When the man did not move but continued to linger near the window, the baker threw down his dough, marched across the shop, and flung open the door. He grabbed the poor man by his collar and demanded, "Pay me."

The startled man said, "Pay you for what?"

"For the smells you have stolen," said the baker.

"Please, sir. I have stolen nothing. I just breathed in the air. Air is free," replied the man.

"It's not free when it's full of the smells from my shop. Pay me now or I will have you arrested!"

When the man did not pay, the baker dragged him through the snow to the magistrate's house. He pounded on the door. After a long time, the magistrate opened the door and peered into the morning light. He was in his nightshirt, and his hair was sticking out from under his nightcap. He was surprised to see the baker holding a struggling man.

"Arrest this thief. Throw him in jail. He stole the smells from my shop," said the baker.

The sleepy judge said, "Come in and tell me the story. But give me time to get dressed."

The judge reappeared with his nightshirt sticking out from under his official robes and his hair sticking out from under his official wig. He had a twinkle in his eye. He sat the men down in his official chambers, where he settled the disputes of the town.

The judge said, "All right, tell me the whole story from beginning to end. Baker, you begin." He listened patiently to the ranting of the aggrieved merchant about the theft of his smells. He listened to the plea of the poor man about free air.

And when he heard all the facts twice, and the men were ready to repeat the tale in even louder voices, the judge called a halt. "Stop! Silence! Just be quiet! I have reached a decision."

"Sir," the judge addressed the poor man. "Do you have any money?" The poor man reached into his pocket and brought out two copper coins of the smallest denomination.

"Please, your honor," said the man. "That's all the money I have in the world."

But the judge held out his hand and said, "Give me your money." The poor man put the coins into the judge's hand.

The judge cleared his throat and announced, "After hearing all the evidence in the aforesaid case, I find that the baker, also called the plaintiff, owned the smells coming from his shop, and that this man, also called the defendant, breathed in these smells without permission or payment. Therefore the baker is entitled to just compensation."

The baker smiled, perhaps for the first time in his adult life, and held out his hand to receive the coins. "It's not the money," said the baker. "It's the principle. Let this be an example."

The baker stood and waited for payment. But the judge did not drop the coins into the open palm. He said, "Listen and listen closely." He shook the coins and they rattled and jingled together. "That is your full payment," pronounced the judge.

The baker challenged the judge, "Give me my coins, Your Honor."

"No," replied the wise magistrate. "Punishment should fit the crime. I have decided that the price for the smell of bread shall be the sound of money." Then the judge returned the coins to the poor man.

So ends the tale of the baker, the poor man, and the judge.

SOURCES:

• Knappert, Jan. "Nuwasi as Cadi." In *Myths and Legends of the Swahili*. Nairobi and London: Heinemann Educational Books, 1970.

• Rugoff, Milton. *A Harvest of World Folk Tales*. New York: Viking Press,

1949. A Frenchman who flavored bread with smoke from a roast had to pay with the sound of money.

- Edmonds, I. G. "Ooka and the Stolen Smell." In *Ooka the Wise: Tales of Old Japan*. Indianapolis, Ind.: Bobbs-Merrill, 1961. Reprint, Camden, Conn.: Linnet Books, 1994. A student living over a tempura shop flavors rice with the smell of food.
- Htin Aung, Maung and Helen G. Trager "A Greedy Stallkeeper and the Poor Traveler." In *A Kingdom Lost for a Drop of Honey and Other Burmese Folktales*. New York: Parents, 1968. The shadow of money is payment for the smell of fish.
- Henius, Frank. "A Baker's Neighbor." In *Stories of the Americas*. Charles Scribner's Sons, 1944. The touch of money is payment for the smell of bread.
- Kelsey, Alice Geer. "The Woodcutter's Helper." In *Once the Hodja*. New York: David McKay Co., Inc., 1945. The sound of money is payment for grunting while another chops wood.
- Abrahams, Roger D. "Rich Man, Poor Man." In *African Folktales*. New York: Pantheon Books, 1983. The sound of a goat bleating is payment for the smell of food.

COMMENTS:

I first heard this tale from storyteller Pat Peterson at the Honey Bear Bakery in Seattle. She said she heard it from Elizabeth Ellis at the National Storytelling Festival in Jonesborough, Tennessee. This type of ear-to-mouth transmission is the basis of storytelling. One storyteller hears a tale and tells it with new embellishments; another teller hears and tells the tale with additional refinements. The story remains alive and fluid in the oral tradition until a folklorist, collector, or editor freezes the story on a page in a book.

Frivolous Lawsuits

The story "The Stolen Smells" demonstrates that frivolous lawsuits have a very old tradition. This judge could have closed his door and refused to hear this frivolous dispute. Perhaps he invited the men inside in order to hear an amusing tale. Perhaps he wanted to prevent a fistfight. Perhaps he did not want to prejudge the dispute until he heard all the facts.

The famous Justice Benjamin Cardozo addressed the issue of frivolous lawsuits in *Morningstar v Lafayette Hotel*, 211 NY 465 (1914). Cardozo was born in New York City in 1870. He served on the New York bench and was appointed to the United States Supreme Court by President Herbert Hoover. He was a modest, polite, and hardworking jurist who is remembered for the brief and lucid writing style of his opinions, as demonstrated in the Morningstar case. Morningstar was a guest at the Lafayette Hotel in Buffalo, New York. He paid for both room and meals. Cardozo wrote:

> He seems to have wearied of the hotel fare, and his yearning for variety has provoked this lawsuit. He went forth and purchased some spareribs, which he presented to the hotel chef with a request that they be cooked for him. This was done, but with the welcome viands there came the unwelcome addition of a bill or check for one dollar, which he was asked to sign. He refused to do so, claiming that the charge was excessive.

Morningstar left after the hotel staff announced publicly that they refused to serve him. He sued the hotel to recover damages for damage to his reputation, and for the refusal to serve him. The lower court ruled against Morningstar, and said the hotel was not required to serve a guest who refused to pay a lawful charge.

Morningstar appealed, and Cardozo ruled that the lower court had made a mistake in allowing testimony that Morningstar was a "kicker," a chronic faultfinder. A new trial was granted, but the outcome is unknown.

Justice Cardozo said, "It is no concern of ours that the controversy at the root of the lawsuit may seem to be trivial." He commented that Morningstar "...chose to resist a wrong which, if it may seem trivial to some, must have have seemed substantial to him." Cardozo also spoke more broadly about seemingly trivial lawsuits:

> To enforce one's rights when they are violated is never a legal wrong, and may often be a moral duty. It happens in many instances that the violation passes with no effort to redress it—sometimes from praiseworthy forbearance, sometimes from weakness, sometimes from mere inertia. But the law, which creates a right, can certainly not concede that an insistence upon its enforcement is evidence of a wrong.

Cardozo quoted Rudolf von Ibering, in his "Struggle of Law," that the development of law is due to the persistence of the individual to resist aggression. Therefore, the individual owes it to himself and society never to permit a legal right to be wantonly infringed.

There has been criticism of Cardozo's indulgent view of frivolous litigation. Critics argue that lawsuits clog the courts, maliciously harass defendants, and cause people to fear being sued (lexiphobia). Courts and legislators have attempted to limit frivolous lawsuits by sanctioning attorneys who file them, and making plaintiffs who lose in court pay the defendant's attorney fees.

A federal judge in Philadelphia tried to stop a woman from filing frivolous suits in 1994. The woman filed more than seven hundred law suits in a year; her convoluted, handwritten complaints did not contain a single complete sentence. She always asked to proceed *in forma pauperis,* which means that she had no money and asked to file without paying a filing fee. The judge ordered that, in the future, her complaints had to be accompanied by the usual one hundred and twenty dollar filing fee, be signed by a lawyer, or include a physician's statement indicating that she is mentally competent.[1]

Solomon's Judgment

❧

(Israel)

Two harlots came to the king, and stood before him. The one woman said, "Oh, my lord, this woman and I dwell in the same house, and I gave birth to a child while she was in the house. Then on the third day after I was delivered, this woman also gave birth, and we were alone; there was no one else with us in the house, only we two were in the house. And this woman's son died in the night, because she lay on it. And she arose at midnight, and took my son from beside me while our maid-servant slept, and laid it in her bosom, and laid her dead son in my bosom. When I rose in the morning to nurse my son, behold, it was dead; but when I looked at it more closely in the morning, behold, it was not the child I had borne."

But the other woman said, "No, the living child is mine, and the dead child is yours."

The first said, "No, the dead child is yours, and the living child is mine." Thus they spoke before the king.

Then the king said, "The one says, 'This is my son that is alive, and your son is dead'; and the other says, 'No, but your son is dead, and my son is the living one.' "

And the king said, "Bring me a sword." So a sword was brought before the king. And the king said, "Divide the living child in two, and give half to the one, and the half to the other."

Then the woman whose son was alive said to the king, because her heart yearned for her son, "Oh my lord, give her the living child, and by no means slay it."

But the other said, "It shall be neither mine nor yours; divide it."

Then the king answered and said, "Give the living child to the first woman, and by no means slay it; she is its mother."

And all Israel heard of the judgment which the king had rendered; and they stood in awe of the king, for they perceived that the wisdom of God was in him to render justice.

SOURCES:

- 1 Kings 3: 16-28. Revised Standard Edition.
- Shannon, George. "Two Mothers." In *Stories to Solve: Folktales from Around the World*. New York: Greenwillow Books, 1985. A king tells two women to pull on the child in a tug-of-war and the woman who pulls hardest wins. The true mother lets go so the child would not be hurt.
- Van Buitemen, J. A. B. "Mahosadha's Judgment." In *Tales of Ancient India*. Chicago: University of Chicago Press, 1959. A tug-of-war test is given to a mother and a red-eyed ghoul.
- Nahmad, H.M. "The Righteous Heir." In *A Portion in Paradise and other Jewish Folktales*. New York: W. W. Norton, 1968. In order to determine the rightful heir, a judge orders the bones of the dead father to be dug up and burned as punishment for not leaving a will. The usurper agrees, but the true son renounces his claim rather than have his father's remains disturbed.

COMMENTS:

Solomon the Wise

*"And all the kings of the earth sought the presence
of Solomon to hear the wisdom that the Lord
had put into his heart."*
(2 Chronicles 9:23)

Nearly all of the known historical facts about Solomon are recorded in the Bible, especially I Kings 1-11 and II Chronicles 1-9. Born about 1,000 B.C., Solomon, the second son of King David and Bathsheba, was selected by his father as his successor to the throne of the united kingdoms of Israel and Judah. During Solomon's forty-year reign, Israel reached its "Golden Age;" construction of public buildings, foreign trade, commercial prosperity, and intellectual activity flourished.

Maritime trading provided cedar from Lebanon and artisans from Phoenicia for Solomon's massive building programs. Solomon forced labor from the Caanites and the Israelites to cut, haul, and lay stone from the mountains. Solomon built the temple in Jerusalem to house the ark of the covenant. The construction took seven years (I Kings 5, 6), but for unknown reasons, the temple sat unused for thirteen years. Then, accompanied by magnificent ceremony and feasting, the ark of the covenant was brought from the tent where it had been kept and placed in the temple. The ark was a chest made of wood and covered with gold. On the top of the ark were two cherubs facing each other with wings touching. Inside were the two stone tablets God had given Moses (I Kings 8:9).

Next, Solomon built the royal palace. Its lofty roof was supported by forty-five pillars of cedar and was probably called "The House of the Forest of Lebanon." In front of the palace was the "Hall of Judgment" or the "King's Gate" where Solomon administered justice.[1]

Solomon was also known for his wise writing. Traditionally, the biblical books Proverbs, Ecclesiastes, and the Song of Solomon have been attributed to him.[2] According to tradition, it was Solomon who first used the parable. The parable, which is so prevalent in Jewish folklore, is an entertaining story that embodies truth and wisdom. Second-century Talmud scholar Rabbi Hanina said, "Until the time of Solomon, the Torah could have been compared to a well full of cool, refreshing water, but because of its extraordinary depth, no one could get to the bottom. What was necessary was to find a rope long enough to tie to the bucket in order to bring up the water. Solomon made up this rope with his parables, and thus enabled everyone to reach to the profoundest depths of the well."[3]

Solomon was a legendary figure, as well as a historical person. According to legend, Solomon had dominion over humans, angels, demons, animals, and birds.[4] For example, he forced the jinn, supernatural beings (sometimes pronounced "genies"), to work for him building the temple. He punished rebellious jinn by putting them in brass bottles and casting them into the sea. In the *Arabian Nights'* tale "The Fisherman and the Genie," a fisherman retrieves such a bottle, unseals it, and unknowingly releases a jinni. The jinni pronounces Solomon as "Suliman, son of Daud."[5]

Solomon could speak the language of animals and birds; they frequently told him information when he was making judgments. For example, in the folktale "Solomon and the Bee," the Queen of Sheba tests the king's wisdom by showing him two bouquets of flowers and asking, "Which is real?" A bee buzzes the correct answer in Solomon's ear.[6]

During Solomon's lifetime, his prestige declined. His extravagance, his policy of forced labor, and the expense of maintaining the court and the armies may have been too much for his people. His fall has been attributed, in part, to his polygamy; Solomon had seven hundred wives and three hundred concubines. Initially, the marriages fostered alliances with foreign nations, but as he grew older, his idleness among his wives compromised his reputation. The Bible reports that after permitting his wives to burn incense and make sacrifices to foreign gods, Solomon incurred divine wrath (I Kings 11:3-13).

Solomon ruled until his death, and was succeeded by his son, Rehoboam. The kingdom split into Israel and Judah. Solomon's Temple was destroyed by Nebuchadnezzar (2 Kings 24:13, 2 Chronicles 36:7). The ark of the covenant was taken to Babylon and was either destroyed or disappeared.[7] All that is left of the glory of Solomon are his words and the stories about him.

Ooka and the Wasted Wisdom

෯

(Japan)

One day a case came to Ooka's court concerning a baby boy. Two women claimed to be its mother, and Ooka was faced with the problem of deciding which woman was telling the truth. Both women had recently come to Yedo (old Tokyo), and so there were no witnesses to support either claim.

Thinking that the child himself would be sure to recognize his own mother, the judge placed him in the middle of the floor, expecting him to crawl toward one of the women. But the child paid no attention to either of the two women, and cried for Ooka to pick him up.

A murmur of amusement ran around the courtroom. Ooka's ears began to turn pink.

The great judge soon thought of another test, however. He ordered the two women to take hold of one of the baby's arms and to pull as hard as they were able.

"I am sure the real mother will be given strength so that she will win the struggle," he explained. What he really expected was the real mother would stop pulling the child, for fear of hurting him.

But the two women were not fooled by Ooka's cleverness, and told the judge they knew he was playing a trick.

Ooka sighed. Finally he called a court attendant and said, "Go buy me a bowl of goldfish, a handful of bamboo sticks, three pieces of

Whitehead called Mr. Stern and threatened to kill herself and the baby if he tried to take custody. Mrs. Whitehead was hospitalized, and the Sterns got physical custody of the baby. After much legal maneuvering and media coverage, a custody hearing was held in a New Jersey Superior Court between Mrs. Whitehead and the Sterns.

Eleven experts testified on the issue of the best interests of the child. There is no set standard for determining the child's interests. However, one of the experts, a psychology professional at a medical center, listed nine comprehensive questions or criteria for defining those best interests:

1. Was the child wanted and planned for?
2. What is the emotional stability of the people in the child's home environment?
3. What is the stability and peacefulness of the families?
4. What is the ability of the subject adults to recognize and respond to the child's physical and emotional needs?
5. What are the family attitudes towards education and their motivation to encourage curiosity and learning?
6. What is the ability of the adults to make rational judgments?
7. What is the capacity of the adults in the child's life to instill positive attitudes about matters concerning health?
8. What is the capacity of the adults in the baby's life to explain circumstances of origin with least confusion and greatest emotional support?
9. Which adults would better help the child cope with her own life?

Using these criteria and other evidence, the trial judge ruled that it was in the best interests of "Baby M" to be placed in her birth father's sole custody. The trial judge ruled that the surrogacy contract was valid, terminated the parental rights of Mrs. Whitehead, and presided over the baby's adoption by Mrs. Stern.[1]

Mrs. Whitehead appealed. The Supreme Court of New Jersey reviewed the record of the trial court and considered whether the court made the errors that Mrs. Whitehead alleged. She said the trial court erred in finding the surrogacy contract was valid, terminating her parental rights, awarding custody to Mr. Stern, and allowing the adoption by Mrs. Stern.

First, a unanimous court overruled the lower court and invalidated the surrogacy contract. Although no laws in New Jersey specifically concerned surrogacy contracts, the court ruled that this contract violated both state law and public policy. In New Jersey, it was illegal to pay or accept money for any adoption. Therefore, the condition that Mr. Stern pay Mrs. Whitehead $10,000 was illegal. Also, under state law a birth mother could not irrevocably agree to surrender the child before the birth. The contract was unenforceable because, even before she was pregnant, Mrs. Whitehead made an irrevocable pledge to relinquish the baby and her parental rights. Finally, the contract was unenforceable because it did not consider the best interest of the child; it took the child from the mother and did not inquire into the suitability of the father to raise the child.

The Supreme Court found that the trial court erred in terminating Mrs. Whitehead's parental rights. New Jersey law allowed termination only where there has been a voluntary surrender of the child to the state, or where there has been a showing of parental abandonment or unfitness. The contract and her promise to relinquish the baby was invalid; Mrs. Whitehead had attempted to revoke her consent by refusing to surrender the baby. Furthermore, the trial court concluded that Mrs. Whitehead was a good mother to her other two children. Consequently, both Mr. Stern and Mrs. Whitehead retained parental rights.

Nonetheless, the Supreme Court upheld the trial court's decision to award custody to Mr. Stern. Evidence given at trial showed the Whitehead family had financial and marital problems, caused in part by

Mr. Whitehead's alcoholism. (After the custody trial and before the appeal was heard, the Whiteheads divorced, and Mrs. Whitehead remarried.) By contrast, the Sterns had a happy marriage, stable personalities, and financial resources. They had no other children, and the little girl was thriving under their care.

However, the Supreme Court ruled that Mrs. Whitehead was entitled to visitation rights; it was in the "best interests of the child" to know her mother. Because visitation was not addressed in the trial court, the higher court remanded the issue back to the trial court for a hearing and determination of what kind of visitation Mrs. Whitehead should be granted.

In conclusion, the New Jersey Supreme Court said the Whitehead-Stern contract was invalid. But until the state legislature made laws considering surrogacy contracts, there was no prohibition against contracts in which the mother received no payment and was given the right to change her mind and assert her parental rights.[2]

As a result of the "Baby M" case, courts and legislatures began examining the issue of surrogacy contracts. As of 1992, sixteen states passed laws restricting surrogacy contracts.[3]

The Warmth of a Fire

❧

(Jewish)

In the old days, when King David ruled, there was a poor man who had a dream of owning his own land. But he was only a servant of a rich merchant. The merchant was so rich that he owned everything he wanted. But he was tired of everything he had, and there was nothing new to amuse him.

One cold night, the merchant called his servant to bring wood for the fire. When the fire was blazing, the merchant asked, "I wonder how much cold can a man stand? Do you think it would be possible for a man to stand all night on the highest peak of a mountain—without blankets or clothing or fire?"

"I don't know," the servant replied. "But it would be a foolish thing to do."

"Perhaps, if he had nothing to gain by it," the merchant said. "But I bet a man couldn't do it."

"Master, I am sure a courageous man could stand naked on the mountain and not die of it. But as for me, it's not my business; I've nothing to bet."

"Well," said the master. "Since you are so sure it can be done, I'll make a bet with you anyway. If you can stand among the rocks at the top of the mountain for an entire night and not die, I will give you ten acres of good farm land with a house and cattle. Remember—no blankets or clothing or fire."

The servant could hardly believe what he heard. "Do you really mean your offer?" he asked.

"I am a man of my word," his master boasted.

"Then tomorrow night I will do it," accepted the poor man. "And afterward, for all the years to come, I shall farm my own land, and be my own master."

But he was worried, because the wind swept bitterly across that peak. He went to his wife and told her of the bet. The wife listened quietly until he had finished; she said, "Husband, I will help you. Tomorrow night, as the sun goes down, I will build a fire at the foot of the mountain. You will be able to see it as you stand on the peak. All night long you must watch the fire and think of its warmth. Think of me, your wife, sitting here tending for you. Think of the land we will farm. Do not close your eyes. Do not let the darkness creep upon you. If you do this you will survive, no matter how bitter the night wind."

The next day the poor man went back to his master's house. His heart was confident. He said, "I am ready." In the afternoon, he went to the mountain and climbed to the top. Servants went to watch him and report to the merchant. As night fell, the poor man took off his clothes and stood in the damp cold wind. At the foot of the mountain, his wife built a fire. It shone like a star in the blackness.

The wind turned colder and passed through his flesh and into the marrow of his bones. The rock on which he stood turned to ice. Each hour the cold numbed him more, until he thought he would never be warm again. He kept his eyes upon the twinkling light far below. He remembered that his wife sat there tending his fire for him. Sometimes wisps of fog blotted out the light, and then he strained to see until the fog passed. He sneezed and coughed and shivered, but he survived. When the dawn came, he put on his clothes and went down the mountain to claim his reward.

The merchant was astonished to see the poor man. He questioned his servants, "Did he stay all night without blankets or clothing or fire?"

"Yes," his servants answered. "He did all of these things."

"Well, you are a strong fellow," the merchant said. "How did you manage to do it?"

"Master, I endured by watching the fire at the foot of the mountain," he said.

"What! You watched a fire? I said no fire. You lose the bet! You own no land! You are still my servant!"

"But, Master, this fire was not close enough to warm me. It was far away."

The merchant said. "You didn't keep the conditions. It was only the fire that saved you."

The poor man was devastated. He went to his wife and told her what had happened.

She advised, "Take the matter to King David."

The poor man went to King David and complained, and the King sent for the merchant. Each man told his story. The servant said once more, "I endured by watching the fire at the foot of the mountain."

King David declared, "I find for the merchant because the servant did not comply with the terms of the wager; he used fire."

As the poor man and his wife left the palace in tears, they met Solomon, the son of King David. "Why do you weep?" he inquired. The poor man told his story.

Solomon said, "Don't worry. Justice will be done."

Some days later, Solomon sent invitations to a feast at the palace. Among the guests, he invited King David, the merchant, and the poor man and his wife. Solomon ordered a lamb to be slaughtered and preparations for the feast to begin.

On the day of the feast, the guests arrived and were seated. Time passed, and no food was served. King David asked his son, "When will the meal begin?"

"When the lamb is roasted," Solomon told his father.

Evening came and the guests began to whisper among themselves. It was very curious that no food was served. King David went to the kitchen to find out about the delay. There he saw a blazing fire in the hearth at one end of the kitchen and at the other end of the kitchen he saw the meat on a table —cold and uncooked. King David summoned his son and asked, "Why did you do this? Why did you invite us to a feast and then not roast the lamb? The fire is at one end and the meat at the other."

Solomon answered, "If the poor man was warmed by the fire at the bottom of the mountain while he stood at the top, then this lamb can be cooked by the fire which is merely across the kitchen."

"My son, you are right," said the King.

Then he ordered the lamb to be put in the fire and roasted. Father and son returned to their guests, and King David filled all the wine glasses. He made a toast, "Here is a salute to my son Solomon, who is wise enough to teach his father about the spirit of the law." Then he told about the dispute over fire and ordered the rich man to award the servant with land, a house, and cattle. When the lamb was roasted, the feast began.

SOURCES:

My version is a blend of these folktales:

- Courlander, Harold and Wolf Leslau. "Fire on the Mountain." In *The Fire on the Mountain and other Ethiopian Stories.* New York: Henry Holt and Co., 1950. A man who loses a bet because he watches fire on a distant mountain rewards the winner with the smell of food.
- Sadeh, Pinhas. "King Solomon and the Poor Man." In *Jewish Folktales.* New York: Doubleday, 1989. A man who loses a bet because he watches a lamp in a window rewards the winner with uncooked lamb,

which the fire across the kitchen should have cooked.

- Kelsey, Alice Geer. "One Candle Power." In *Once the Hodja*. New York: David McKay Co., Inc., 1994. A candle should cook the contents of a kettle.

The Fisherman and the King's Chamberlain

◈

(Burma)

Once there was a King who could not eat any meal unless it included a dish of fried fish. One day, there blew a great storm, and fishermen could not catch any fish. The King could not eat any breakfast because there was no fried fish, and he was very annoyed. Lunchtime came, but there was no fish, and the King was very angry. Dinnertime approached, but still there was no prospect of any fried fish, and the King was now desperate. "Let it be announced by beat of gong and drum," ordered he, "that the fisherman who brings me but one single fish will be given any reward that he may name." However, the storm continued to rage, and the waters remained turbulent.

At last at dusk, a Fisherman, trying with a mere line and hook, caught a fat and oily fish, and he ran with all his might to the King's palace. The guards, seeing the fish in the Fisherman's hand, threw open the gates, and the Fisherman reached the King's chamber without hindrance. But at the chamber door, the Chamberlain said, "Promise me half your reward and I will let you in."

"One-tenth," promised the Fisherman.

"Oh, no," said the Chamberlain, "One half, and no less."

"Agreed," replied the Fisherman, and in great glee, the Chamberlain announced to the King the arrival of a Fisherman with a fish. The King, in great joy, seized hold of the fish, and the Fisherman's hand, and rushed into the kitchen.

After the fish had been fried, the dinner laid before the King, and the King had eaten, he sat back hugging his well-filled stomach, and asked, "Fisherman, name your reward. Do you want to have a priceless ruby, or a well-paid post, or a pretty maid from the queen's bower?"

"No, Sire, no, Sire," replied the Fisherman, falling on his knees. "I want twenty lashes with your cane."

"The poor fellow is flabbergasted," mused the King, "and he does not know what he is saying." So he said gently to to the Fisherman, "My man, you mean twenty rubies, or twenty elephants, or even twenty horses."

"No, Sire, no, Sire," replied the Fisherman. "I want just twenty lashes with your cane."

"I am sorry," sighed the King, "But I must keep my promise and give you what you ask." So saying, he took up a cane and beat the Fisherman gently.

"No, Sire, no Sire," said the Fisherman, "not so soft, Sire, please hit me hard." The King, feeling annoyed, wielded the cane with some vigor, but when he had given the Fisherman ten lashes, to his astonishment he saw the Fisherman jump away.

"Have I hit you too hard?" the King inquired with concern and pity.

"No, Sire, no, Sire," explained the Fisherman, "but the remaining ten lashes are your Chamberlain's share."

The poor Chamberlain now had to confess what he had done, but pleaded, "My Lord, I asked for a half share of his reward, and not of his punishment."

"But this is my reward and not my punishment," argued the Fisher-man. The King sent for the Princess Learned-in-the-Law to come and decide the case.

"My Lord King," said the Princess Learned-in-the-Law after she had arrived and listened to the two litigants. "The Chamberlain and the Fisherman were partners in a business, to wit, to supply a fish to the King, and they agreed to share. But my Lord, in a partnership, the agreement to share does not mean that only the profits are to be shared, but it means that gain and loss, income and expenditure, success and failure, reward and punishment, are to be equally shared."

The King accepted the judgment of the Princess, and gave the Chamberlain ten good lashes with his cane. Then he said, "The partnership is now dissolved, as the business has ended. As a consequence, however, I order that the Chamberlain be dismissed for corruption and disloyalty, and the Fisherman appointed in his place."

SOURCE:

- Htin Aung, Maung. *Burmese Law Tales; The Legal Element in Burmese Folk-lore.* London: Oxford University Press, 1962. By permission of Oxford University Press.

COMMENTS:

Burmese Law Tales

In his extensive introduction to *Burmese Law Tales,* Maung Htin Aung explains the Juristic tales, or law tales, which are part of the Burmese folk tradition. A Juristic tale demonstrates a legal principle; for example, "The Fisherman and the King's Chamberlain" deals with partnerships and the point of law that partners share in both losses and gains. A law tale could come from many sources: a folktale, a recounting of an actual case, or a Jataka, a Buddhist Birth story. A Juristic tale could be quoted by a litigant in court. The tales also served as examples for the honorary judges appointed by the King to preside in the villages. The Princess Learned-in-the-Law is a folktale character in the Juristic tales who announces the principle of law.[1]

United States Case Study

In a sense, current American law schools also teach legal principles with storytelling. However, spoken folktales are not used. Instead, modern law students study actual cases from casebooks. The case method of instruction was first used by Christopher Columbus Langdell at Harvard University in the late nineteenth century.[2] A case is a judicial decision that is written by an appellate judge after a trial has taken place and the decision appealed. A case contains the facts of the dispute, the applicable law, the application of the law to the facts, and a ruling or finding.

Before class, students study a case and write a "brief" (a summary of the facts, law, and finding). Then in class, the law instructor questions students about the case and how the finding might change if the facts are changed. The instructor does not lecture, but uses the Socratic Method that allows the students to find their own answers through reasoning and dialogue.

Law school is a three-year course of study which has a standard curriculum including constitutional law, trusts and estates, and criminal law. To be accepted to law school, a student must have a four-year degree, good grades, and score well on the Law School Admission Test. After law school is completed, a lawyer must pass a bar exam in the state where a practice will be established.

Ali Cogia, Merchant of Baghdad

❧

(Arabia)

Long ago in Baghdad there lived a merchant named Ali Cogia. He had no wife or child. He made a modest profit and lived a modest life.

One night he dreamed his father appeared to him and scolded him because he had not made a pilgrimage to Mecca, as is the duty of a good Muslim. Ali Cogia woke from the dream and said, "My father is right, but how can I leave? Who will tend my shop? Who will take care of my house?"

But the dream occurred again and again until Ali Cogia knew he would not sleep soundly until he made a pilgrimage to Mecca. He sold all his wares, his shop, and his small house. He received over a thousand pieces of gold. "I will take some gold for the journey, but where can I leave the rest?"

When he thought of a plan, he put the coins in a large jar and filled the rest of the jar with olives. He carried the jar to the neighboring merchant. "My old friend, you have probably heard that I am leaving for Mecca in a few days. Could you keep this jar of olives for me until I come back?"

The merchant replied, "Of course, here is the key to my shop. Take the jar into the shop. Put it wherever you like. I promise that you shall find it in the same place when you get back."

Ali Cogia put the jar in a dusty corner of a back room, said his goodbyes, and joined a caravan to Mecca. He liked traveling so much that after his visit to the mosque in Mecca, he bought some goods with his remaining gold coins, and joined a caravan to Cairo. He sold his goods in Egypt, and journeyed to visit the Pyramids and the Nile river. Next he met some merchants on their way to India. He joined them. So it was that Ali Cogia traveled and traded for seven years. One day he said, "I am tired of traveling. I long for Baghdad. And with my thousand pieces of gold that I left in the olive jar, I can buy a new shop and live out my life in the city where I was born."

On the very day that Ali Cogia decided to return home, his friend's wife remarked, "I have been craving olives all day. If only I had some olives, I would be content."

The merchant remembered the jar left by Ali Cogia. "There are olives in the back room. Ali Cogia left them with me. But he has been gone for seven years. Surely he is dead. So bring a lamp—I will fetch them, and we will see if they are still fit to eat."

"Oh, no, husband. Ali Cogia may return any day. It would be shameful to betray your trust. Do not pay attention to my idle words; I have no desire for olives."

But the merchant got a lamp and found the olive jar. He broke the seal on the top and pulled out the cork. The topmost olives were rotten, so he scooped them out and reached deep into the bottom to see if the remaining olives were in better condition. He pulled out a handful of olives, and also found a piece of gold. He did not tell his wife what he found. Instead he told her, "The olives are all rotten. I recorked the jar."

When his wife was asleep, he crept into the back room and emptied the jar. "So much gold! All for me!" He hid the money. The next day he went out and bought fresh olives, filled the jar, and sealed it. Then he put the vase in the same spot where Ali Cogia had left it.

Only a few days later, Ali Cogia re-entered Baghdad. He went to see his old friend the merchant, who received him with open arms. "Welcome back, Ali Cogia. We feared you were dead."

"Allah be praised, I am well. And I am blessed to have a friend like you. Could you please give me the jar of olives that you have been so kind to care for?"

"Oh, yes, dear friend," said the merchant. "Here is the key to my shop. The jar is where you put it."

Ali Cogia unlocked the shop, went to the spot where he put the jar, and pulled the cork out. He thrust his hand to the bottom. There was no gold!

Ali Cogia ran to the merchant's house. "My friend," he cried, "my thousand pieces of gold are gone. Perhaps you might have borrowed it for your business purposes. If that is so, you are most welcome. I only ask you give me a receipt. Then you can repay at your leisure."

"Ali Cogia, what gold are you talking about? I gave you the key to my shop; you placed the jar there yourself. Did you not find it in the same spot? I have not touched your jar."

"Please, old friend, I love peace. Don't make me call the law. Give me my gold."

"Ali Cogia, a crowd is gathering, even the children are listening. Please go away."

By this time, neighbors, children, and merchants were listening to the dispute. Ali Cogia turned and laid his cause before them. He showed them the vase of olives. The crowd said, "Merchant, what do you have to say for yourself?"

"Friends, it is true I kept the vase in my shop for seven years. But I swear I did not open it."

Ali Cogia challenged the merchant, "Will you dare repeat your story before the cadi?"

"I would like nothing better. Let's go."

The two men presented themselves to the cadi and told their stories. The cadi asked Ali Cogia, "Do you have witnesses that saw you put the gold in the vase?"

"No, I did it in secret," the man replied.

Without a moment's thought the cadi said, "I find for the merchant." And the merchant returned home in triumph.

Ali Cogia vowed to appeal to the caliph. He drew up a petition, and waited alongside the road where the caliph walked after midday prayer. The caliph heard the petition and granted an audience the next morning.

Later that evening, the caliph went out for a stroll through the town. He was in disguise so he could pass unnoticed through the crowds. He heard children talking. "Let's play being the cadi of Baghdad," said the children. The caliph looked into the courtyard and saw the children gathered in the moonlight.

The smartest and quickest child said, "I will be the cadi. Bring me Ali Cogia and the merchant. I will settle the question of the thousand pieces of gold." The caliph remembered the petition he had read that morning, and he listened with interest to what the children said.

The children liked the game, and they decided the part each would play. The child cadi solemnly took his seat. The child Ali Cogia and the child merchant came forward. Ali Cogia made a low bow. "Please hear my plea. This merchant kept the gold pieces I hid in a vase of olives." He told the entire story he had heard from the real Ali Cogia.

The boy cadi said, "Merchant, tell me your side of the story." The boy merchant repeated all the reasons the real merchant had given to the Cadi of Baghdad. "I never opened the vase in seven years," he responded.

Instead of finding for the merchant, the boy cadi asked a question, "Where is the vase of olives? Bring it to me."

The children pretended to carry a vase and put it at the feet of the boy cadi. "Open the vase."

The children pretended to open the vase. The cadi pretended to eat one. "What good olives. Such bright color and good taste. It seems odd that olives that are seven years old would be so good. Bring me some olive merchants."

Two children came forward as olive merchants. The boy cadi questioned them, "How long can olives be stored and remain good?"

"Three years," said the olive merchants. "After that, they lose color and taste and are only fit to be thrown away."

"Merchants, examine the olives in this vase."

The children pretended to examine the olives. "My lord, these are fresh olives, not even a year old."

The merchant tried to protest, but the boy cadi said, "Be silent. You are a thief. Take him to prison."

So the play ended, and the children all clapped and led the criminal away to prison. The caliph was amazed. "Can there be any better judgment? I will follow this example." He commanded his servants to summon the parties, plus two olive merchants and the boy who acted as cadi. "Instruct Ali Cogia to bring the vase of olives. We will be ready to see justice done. And the cadi will learn from the mouth of a child."

The next morning the boy came to the palace in his finest clothes. The caliph said, "Last night, I overhead your judgment in the case of the stolen gold. I am pleased with the way you conducted the trial. Come seat yourself next to me. Today you will see the real Ali Cogia and the real merchant."

The parties came and bowed before the throne. The caliph said, "Cadi, observe!" To the parties, the caliph commanded, "Now speak. This child will give you justice."

Ali Cogia and the merchant told their stories. Then, just as the night before, the boy said, "Bring me the vase of olives." The boy, the caliph, and the olive merchants tasted the olives. "These olives are fresh and good; they could not have been kept in the vase for seven years," pronounced the olive merchants.

The boy looked at the caliph and said, "My lord, this is not a game now, it is for you, not me, to condemn the merchant."

The caliph stood. "Merchant, you are a thief; you emptied the vase to take the gold. Then you filled the jar with fresh olives. You will go to prison, but first you will tell the place where you hid Ali Cogia's gold."

The merchant told the hiding place and went to prison.

The caliph scolded the cadi for his incompetence. "Learn from the wisdom of this child," he said. Last of all, he sent the boy home with one hundred pieces of silver as a mark of his favor.

SOURCES:

• Lang, Andrew. "Ali Cogia, A Merchant of Bagdad." In *Arabian Nights*. New York: David McKay Co., 1898, reprinted 1967.

• Townsend, George. "The Story of Ali Cogia, A Merchant of Bagdad." In *The Arabian Nights' Entertainments*. New York: Hurd and Houghton, 1873.

• Gilstrap, Robert, and Irene Estabrook. "The Thousand Pieces of Gold." In *The Sultan's Fool and Other North African Tales*. New York: Holt, Rinehart and Winston, 1958.

• Patai, Raphael. "The Gold and The Honey." In *The Gates of the Old City, A Book of Jewish Legends*. Northvale, N. J.: Jason Aronson Inc., 1980. A woman hides gold at the bottom of a honey jar and leaves it with a friend. When she returns from her trip and discovers the missing gold, she appeals to King Saul. When Saul rules against her, David the shepherd boy wins justice by breaking the honey jar and finding two gold pieces stuck to the shards.

Also Sadeh, Pinhas. "King Soloman and the Jar of Honey." In *Jewish Folktales*. New York: Doubleday, 1983.

The Quality of Mercy

❧

(Morocco)

In ancient times, in Morocco and in the city of Casablanca, there was a rich and prominent merchant. One day the merchant fell ill and saw that he would not recover. He called for his only son and asked, "Son, what will you do with my money after I die?"

The son replied, "If anyone needs money, I will give him some. If anyone invites me to a party, I will go. What else is money for?"

The father groaned, "I should have taught you my business and how to make money grow. I was always too busy." The father died knowing that his fortune would be scattered to the winds.

And so it was, the son squandered his inheritance on gifts and celebrations. When he had no roof for his head or food for his belly, he went to the marketplace to beg alms. He sat among the leather workers and the vegetable sellers with his outstretched hand. But on every corner were customers and friends of his father. He was ashamed to be seen begging. "I will go to Marrakesh. No one knows me there," he told himself.

He walked barefoot from the coast of the Atlantic across the rising and falling waves of sand dunes. At last, rising out of the desert like a mirage, he saw the minaret on the red ramparts of Marrakesh. Behind the city towered the snowy range of the Atlas mountains. He walked through olive and palm groves into the city. "Surely I will find my fortune here," he thought.

But because he knew no work but begging, he was soon sitting in the square, surrounded by the music of cymbal and drum. The square was filled with fire-eaters, storytellers, watersellers, and traveling merchants.

One day, a man stopped and called the young beggar by name. "Is it you? Why are you begging?" He was a rich merchant and rival to his late father.

The young man was too ashamed to tell that he had spent his inheritance. Instead he lied. "I was traveling to buy goods! But thieves robbed me."

The rich merchant took pleasure in seeing his rival's son begging for coins. But he put on a kind face and said, "In your father's memory, I will help you. Come and share a glass of mint tea with me."

When they were seated on cushions inside the merchant's stall, the merchant made an astounding offer. "I shall lend you any sum you ask for. You can do whatever you wish with it; any profit you make will be yours. But there is a condition. If at the year's end you do not pay, I will cut one kilogram of flesh from your body."

The young man was startled by the condition of the bargain. But he said, "I have no choice," and signed the agreement.

Throughout the year the young man engaged in business, but he was unlucky and untrained. He lost all the money. What did the young man do? At the end of the year, he went to the palace where the king sat in assembly. He sat outside the gates wringing his hands and rocking to and fro. He took no food or water and prayed he would die before his life was forfeit. He wept, "I should have been born a kitten and drowned at birth."

Days passed. Finally he was observed by the king's daughter. She was on her way to listen to the cases brought before her father. The princess had a quick and clever mind, a tender heart, and a voice as sweet as a flute echoing through marble halls. Her mother and sisters stayed cloistered behind harem walls. Instead the princess went to hear her father's judgments. She concealed herself in a room near the throne to listen to the proceedings. How wise and just was her father—always following the letter of the law.

So it was that one day the princess saw the young man outside the gate, and she was touched by his despair. She sent her servant to ask, "Young man, why do you weep?"

It was not until the third day that the young man replied, "Because I was foolish, and tomorrow I shall die for it." He told his story. When the servant told the princess, she sent a note which said, "Come to court tomorrow, and you will be aided by one who loves mercy."

The appointed hour came. The princess disguised herself as a lawyer. She walked through arched corridors hung with silver lamps and entered the Royal Audience Chamber. The merchant and the young man were assembled with the crowds of petitioners. At last, the King asked the rich merchant, "What does the young man owe you?"

The merchant took the agreement out of his pocket. The King read it and asked the young man, "Do you agree that you signed this document?"

"Ruler of the stars, what can I say? You see my signature here. But one thing you must know. I entered into this agreement because I had no other choice."

Then the Princess stepped from the crowd. She was dressed in a hooded caftan and kept her face turned and concealed in the hood. In a clear, strong voice, she addressed the King, "Our gracious lord! This was a bargain freely made. I agree, on behalf of my client, to give a kilogram of flesh to the merchant, but I insist that he cut off exactly one kilogram in a single stroke. If he cuts off too little, then he must make up the difference, and if he cuts off too much, he must restore the extra amount from his own body."

The merchant protested, "I demand justice! I cannot cut exactly one kilogram of flesh in a single stroke. The agreement does not specify a single stroke."

"That is correct," the princess said. "There is no such condition, but our most wise ruler, in his mercy, may impose one."

"Why should I impose a condition that is impossible, then the merchant is without his money or the flesh?" responded the King.

She answered his question, "The law would require that the merchant receive his payment, either money or flesh. Since there is no money, it is the flesh. And indeed, the merchant has come with a sharpened dagger beneath his robes. But where is the mercy in such a result? The young man will die; the merchant will have only a lump of flesh. And, you, my gracious lord, will have blood on your white marble floors."

She continued, "Perhaps there is another way, a way that provides justice and more kindness than justice requires."

The crowds were hushed and listening to the beardless young lawyer. The King leaned forward. "Counselor, would you enlighten us all about this other way."

"Yes, my lord. Let the merchant receive the labor of the young man until the debt is paid. The young man needs the guidance of a mentor. The merchant needs to temper his ethics with concern for more than money. All can gain from such a result."

"Well spoken!" replied the King. "And so it will be. Young debtor, use this opportunity to make something of yourself. Merchant, you shall take this young debtor into your service. Work and train him until the debt is discharged. It is our wish that you open your heart and mind to him, that you treat him as a son and bring him to the marketplace as a credit to you, his dead father, and your king."

The litigants dropped to the floor and bowed to their king, arose and turned to leave the courtroom. As the crowd filed from the chamber, the King called to the Princess, "Counselor, I wish to speak to you. I do not know you. Come closer so I may see your face."

The Princess was startled and replied, without thinking, "Oh, Father, I cannot." When she realized her slip, she felt exposed and covered her face.

The King roared, "Who is this who calls me 'Father'? Why are you hiding your face? Show yourself."

The Princess turned her face and dropped her hand and hood so that her Father could gaze upon her. "Is this my daughter? What am I to do with such boldness? Leave me!"

The princess fled to the garden when she sat rocking and trembling.

The King paced and pondered and at last went to the garden. He took his daughter's hands and said, "My daughter, my dove. I want to open my heart and mind to you. Will you come and sit at my right hand? Will you be my mercy?"

"Yes, my lord and gracious King," replied the princess. "I will."

Through the long years ahead, the kingdom was ruled with more kindness than justice required.

SOURCES:

- Noy, Dov. "The Cruel Creditor and the Judge's Wise Daughter." In *Moroccan Jewish Folktales.* New York: Herzl Press, 1966.

- Sadeh, Pinhas. "The Young Man and the Lawyer Who Was a Princess." In *Jewish Folktales.* New York: Doubleday, 1989. The editor credits an oral story from Morocco.

- Pino-Saaverdra, Yolando. "White Onion." In *Folktales of Chile.* Chicago: University of Chicago Press, 1967.

- William Shakespeare. *The Merchant of Venice.* Shakespeare's play may have been based on the traditional Jewish folktale. The following is Portia's famous speech in defense of her lover, Antonia, who had contracted a pound of flesh to Shylock:

> *The quality of mercy is not strain'd.*
> *It droppeth as the gentle rain from heaven*
> *Upon the place beneath. It is twice bless'd:*
> *It blesseth him that gives and him that takes.*
> *'Tis mightiest in the mightiest; it becomes*
> *The throned monarch better than his crown.*
> *His scepter shows the force of temporal power,*
> *The attribute to awe and majesty,*
> *Wherein doth sit the dread and fear of kings;*
> *But mercy is above this scepted sway;*
> *It is enthroned in the hearts of kings;*
> *It is an attribute to God himself,*
> *And earthly power doth then show likest God's*
> *When mercy seasons justice.*

COMMENTS:

In retelling folktales, I use my own words and images, but respect the theme and plot of tales that have endured for generations. "The Quality of Mercy" is an exception. My version is not a folktale because I rewrote it extensively to tell at a banquet for the organization of Washington Women Lawyers. In addition, the language is more literary than the simple language of folktales. Consequently, "The Quality of Mercy" is a literary tale based on folk material.

I was attracted to this tale because I love Shakespeare's *The Merchant of Venice*. Also, the tale had a woman appearing in court. However, I did not like the traditional ending in which the heroine wins the case for her lover and the young debtor gets off debt free. Wanting a fair result, I decided to change the ending so the debtor had to repay the money. In the original versions, the princess, as a woman, was excluded from the legal process and had to disguise herself as a man. So I also rewrote the folktale to have the King/Father include his daughter in the legal decisions. This ending is fantasy, because, in reality, throughout history, women have been excluded from the legal process. As the following comments on women's rights demonstrate, American women were not invited to participate, but had to wage a long battle for inclusion in the legal system.

The Women's Rights Movement in the United States: Voting Rights

Until 1920, women were not allowed to vote in the United States. The struggle for voting rights began in colonial days. During the drafting of the Declaration of Independence, Abigail Adams wrote to her husband, John Adams, to "remember the ladies, and be more generous and favorable to them than your ancestors."[1] However, women were not allowed to vote under the Declaration of Independence or the Articles of Confederation.

Later, when the body of the United States Constitution was written, there was no explicit right to vote included. The states were allowed to decide voting qualifications. For all practical purposes, the right to vote was restricted to white males.[2]

A beginning point for women's voting rights was in 1848 when the Seneca Falls Convention was held in upstate New York to discuss "the social, civil and religious rights of women." As a result of a small announcement in the local paper, sixty-eight women and thirty-two men gathered, and signed a Declaration of Principles modeled after the Declaration of Independence. It read in part, "We hold these truths to be self-evident that all men and women are created equal..."[3]

Subsequent meetings called for expanded rights for women. Members of the suffrage movement, believing that women's rights and slavery were connected, were also active in the abolition of slavery. During the Civil War, women put aside concern for their voting rights to back the Thirteenth Amendment to the Constitution to abolish slavery. Women hoped they had been given the right to vote by the Equal Protection Clause of the Fourteenth Amendment, Section 1:

> All persons born or naturalized in the United States and subject to the jurisdiction thereof, are citizens of the United States and of the State wherein they reside. No State shall make or enforce any law which shall abridge the privileges or immunities of citizens of the United States. However, in a series of cases, the Supreme Court found that Section 1 of the Fourteenth Amendment did not expand or protect women's rights.[4]

On November 5, 1872, Susan B. Anthony voted in Rochester, New York. She was arrested and tried in federal court for "unlawful voting." She was tried before a jury of men because women were not allowed to serve on juries; she could not testify on her behalf because women were not allowed to testify. Before the judge directed the jury to deliver a guilty verdict, he stated that the right to vote was given by the State, not the Constitution of the United States:

> If the State of New York should provide that no person should vote until he had reached the age of thirty-one years, or after he had reached the age of fifty, or that no person having gray hair, or who had not the use of all his limbs, should be entitled to vote, I do not see how it could be held to be a violation of any right derived or held under the Constitution of the United States.[5]

Anthony was found guilty and fined one hundred dollars, which she never paid.

Gradually, eleven states gave full voting rights to women. In 1917, the suffrage amendment was passed by the United States House of Representatives; eighteen months later, the amendment was approved by the Senate. The Nineteenth Amendment, which was ratified by the states in 1920, stated:

> The right of citizens of the United States to vote shall not be denied or abridged by the United States or by any state on account of sex.

Women Attorneys

As with the right to vote, women had a similar struggle for the right to practice law. For example, Myra Bradwell was refused admission to the Illinois Bar because she was a woman. In 1873, she appealed to the Supreme Court of the United States, and was told that citizenship did not include the right to practice law. The justice who wrote the opinion, which is often referred to as the "Divine Law of the Creator," stated:

> The paramount destiny and mission of woman are to ful-
> fill the noble and benign offices of wife and mother. This is
> the law of the Creator.[6]

In the same year, another woman, Belva Ann Lockwood, was admitted to the state bar in Washington, D.C. At the time, women were still not allowed to vote or to sit on juries. The legal basis of the inferior status of women was the English common law. The English common law had been brought to America with the colonists and became the legal code of most states. Common law declared: "Husband and wife are one and he is the one." It was both law and custom that a woman was to obey her husband.[7]

Shortly after Lockwood was admitted to the bar, she defended a penniless young woman who was charged with shooting a policeman.

Fortunately, the policeman only had a slight wound.

When Lockwood went to the jail, the woman was hysterical. "I am guilty, I am guilty, I shot him, I shot him." Lockwood calmed the woman and questioned her. Her husband was both a burglar and a robber. One night, a constable came to their house with a search warrant. When he pounded on the door and demanded admittance, the husband handed his wife a loaded gun. "Stay here and shoot if he comes in," the husband commanded before he fled. The wife stood in the hall with the gun pointed at the door. When the constable broke in, she pulled the trigger.

"Let me confess," the wife pleaded with Lockwood.

The attorney advised her not to plead guilty, "We will make the prosecution prove the charge against you."

During the trial, the wife barely maintained control of her emotions. Suddenly, she burst into tears and ran to the empty witness stand.

"I shot him," she sobbed. "I only wanted to save my husband."

The entire story came tumbling out. The prosecution made closing arguments and called for a guilty verdict. Lockwood did not know what to say to the all-male jury. Thinking about the common law gave Lockwood inspiration; when she stood for closing arguments, she said:

> Gentlemen of the jury. My client shot a constable. She admitted it. The District of Columbia is under common law. Laws must be enforced. It is against the law to shoot a man. It is also against the law for a wife to disobey her husband. My client's husband told her to shoot the constable when he came into the house. She obeyed him. Surely you would not have a woman resist her husband's command. Gentlemen, remember the law: husband and wife are one and he is the one. And the husband is the one who is guilty.

The jury brought in a verdict of not guilty. [8]

In recent years, the number of women in the legal profession has dramatically increased; in 1970, there were 9,103 women out of 355,242 lawyers. In 1988, 116,421 lawyers out of 606,768 were women.[9] In addition, in 1989, 40.8 percent of law school graduates were women.[10]

Equal Rights Amendment

An Equal Rights Amendment for Women was introduced into Congress in 1923. It read: "Equality of rights under the law shall not be denied or abridged by the United States or any State on account of sex." The amendment was introduced and ignored in Congress for every year until 1970, when the House of Representatives passed it. In 1972, the Senate also voted for it. But the Amendment was only ratified within the seven-year time limit by thirty-five of the thirty-eight states required.[11] Therefore, the Equal Rights Amendment did not pass to become part of the constitution.

The Pear Seed

&

(China)

Once, in China, there lived a poor man. One day, he was so hungry that his stomach overruled his conscience and he stole a pear in the marketplace. The vendor had him arrested. When the thief was brought to the Emperor for punishment, he said, "If you will pardon me, I will give you a precious gift."

The Emperor looked at the thief's ragged clothes and responded, "What could you possibly have that I would consider precious?"

The thief pulled a small brown pear seed from his pocket, "When this pear seed is planted, it will sprout overnight. It will bear a fruit of gold."

"Plant it," replied the Emperor. "Tomorrow, when I see the golden pear, I will pardon you."

The thief was allowed to go to the garden and dig a hole while all the court watched. "Plant the seed," the Emperor commanded.

"I cannot; I am a thief. This magic seed can only be planted by a person who has never stolen, cheated, or spoken an untruth. Your Majesty, you may have the honor of planting the seed."

The Emperor blushed, stammered, and blustered, "I am the Emperor; I do not plant crops. Give the seed to the Prime Minister."

The Prime Minister refused, "I am very bad at growing things. I could not grow even a magic seed. Give the seed to the Royal Treasurer."

The Royal Treasurer also gave an excuse. One by one, all the officials in the court declined to plant the pear seed. Everyone stood before the empty hole in silence. Finally, the thief spoke, "Not one of you can plant the seed because not one of you is without a lie, a theft, a misdeed. Yet I am to be punished for stealing one piece of fruit when I was hungry. Is that justice?"

The Emperor replied, "Justice demands that you be released." And so it was.

SOURCES:

- Wyndham, Robert. "The Marvelous Pear Seed." In *Tales People Tell in China*. New York: Julian Messner, 1971.
- Rugoff, Milton. "The Wise Rogue." In *A Harvest of World Folk Tales*. New York: Viking Press, 1949.
- Livo, Norma J. "The Old Thief." In *Who's Afraid...? Facing Children's Fears with Folktales*. Englewood, Colo.: Teacher Ideas Press, 1994.

COMMENTS:

This story has a variety of meanings; one is that, if we want lawfulness and justice, we must examine our own thoughts and actions. Also, this story tells us to not to think of and treat a wrongdoer as someone totally alien to ourselves. The New Testament has a story with a similar message:

> Jesus was sitting in the temple, teaching to a crowd of people. The scribes and Pharisees brought a woman and stood her in front of Jesus. They said, "Teacher, this woman has been caught in the act of adultery. Now in the law Moses commanded us to stone such. What do you say about her?"
>
> They were testing Jesus, so they could bring some charge against him if he answered incorrectly. But Jesus stooped

down, and wrote on the ground with his finger, as though he did not hear them.

When they continued asking him, he stood up and said, "Let him that is without sin among you be the first to cast a stone at her." Again he stooped down, and wrote on the ground.

One by one, they left until Jesus was left alone with the woman. He stood and said unto her, "Woman, where are they? Has no one condemned you?"

She said, "No one, Lord."

And Jesus said, "Neither do I condemn you; go, and do not sin again."

—John 7: 53, Revised Standard Version

privilege of being my dinner."

"No, no! Do not eat me, Señor Snake!" cried the Rabbit, who was backed up against the mountain.

"Si, si!" said the Snake, following the Rabbit and keeping his snake eyes fixed firmly upon him. "You must have your reward, and I must have my dinner."

At this very moment, and just in the nick of time, Coyote appeared.

"What goes on here?" he demanded. Both the Rabbit and the Snake began talking at the same time. "Señor Snake is trying to eat me," said Rabbit. "Señor Rabbit tried to kill me," protested Rattlesnake. "Someone is not telling the truth," declared Coyote. Rabbit and Rattlesnake were willing for Señor Coyote to act as judge and settle the dispute.

Rabbit said. "I came here and found Señor Snake under this stone. I pushed it off him and he promised me a reward. But I ask no reward; all I want is my life. He wants to eat me up. That is to be my reward. Is that fair?"

"Completely untrue," the Snake responded. "What Señor Rabbit says is not what happened. I was sleeping in the sun at the foot of this mountain. He pushed the stone on me and was leaving me to die. I escaped and now, I have the right to eat him. Isn't that fair?"

Judge Coyote thought and thought. He looked first to the Rabbit and then to the Snake. "Let us see. Friends, we must settle this matter correctly. Now, both of you are agreed that Señor Snake was under the stone. Is it not so?"

"Si," said the Rattlesnake.

"Si," said the Rabbit. "That is so."

Coyote continued, "I must know now just how everything was. Señor Snake, will you please move over here next to the stone, and Señor Rabbit and I will roll it back on top of you. Then, I can decide this dispute correctly."

The snake agreed and moved next to the stone. Rabbit and Coyote rolled the stone back upon the snake's back. "Ouch!" said Rattlesnake.

"Now," said Coyote, "is that the way you were, Señor Snake?"

"Yes, this is the way I was," the Rattlesnake, squirming in discomfort.

"Can you get out?" asked Coyote.

"No," said Rattlesnake.

"Are you sure you can't get out?" asked Coyote again.

"I'm sure I can't get out!" said Rattlesnake.

"And that is the way you will stay," said Judge Coyote. "You are the great villain of the animalitos. I know you are lying, because I never heard of a rabbit trying to kill a snake. But I often heard of a snake trying to eat a rabbit. Now you have your reward for trying to eat Señor Rabbit after he treated you with kindness." Coyote and Rabbit walked away and left Rattlesnake under the rock. For all I know, he may be there still.

SOURCES:

- West, J. Frank; Mody C. Boatwright; and Harry O. Ransom. "Señor Coyote Acts as Judge." In *Coyote Wisdom*. Dallas and Austin: Texas Folklore Society, 1938. Facsimile edition: Southern Methodist University Press, 1965.

- Edmonds, I. G. "Señor Coyote and the Tricked Trickster." In *Trickster Tales*. New York: J. B. Lippincott, 1966. A Mexican story in which mouse finds coyote in a trap. Mouse frees coyote in exchange for coyote's promise to be a servant. Coyote wins freedom by tricking snake back under the rock after mouse's father rolled the rock off snake.

- West, John O. "Senor Coyote Acts as Judge." In *Mexican-American*

Folklore. Little Rock, Ark.: August House, 1988.

• Peck, Leigh. *Don Coyote*. Eau Claire, Wisc.: E. M. Hale and Company.

• Zong, In-Sob. "Ungrateful Tiger." In *Folk Tales from Korea*. London: Routledge & Kegan Paul Ltd., 1952.

COMMENTS:

Character Evidence

In this tale, Judge Coyote was presiding over a trial for attempted murder. His task was to decide whether it was Rattlesnake or Rabbit who tried to kill the other. In making his decision, he considered their character. Coyote took judicial notice of the everyday knowledge that rattlesnakes kill and rabbits don't.

Character evidence is evidence about a person's disposition or traits, such as honesty. During a criminal trial, evidence of the accused's bad character may not be introduced to help prove the accused's propensity to commit the crime charged.[1] For example, during a trial for theft, a prosecutor generally can not introduce evidence of the defendant's past thievery in order to show "Once a thief, always a thief." As Federal Rule of Evidence 404(b) indicates:

> Evidence of other crimes, wrongs, or acts is not admissible to prove the character of a person in order to show that he acted in conformity therewith. It may, however, be admissible for other purposes, such as proof of motive, opportunity, intent, preparation, plan, knowledge, identity or absence of mistake or accident.

There are two reasons character evidence is inadmissible to prove the crime charged. First, the pattern of bad conduct may not be relevant to the crime charged. Second, even if there was relevancy, it is outweighed by the prejudice the character evidence generates against the defendant. When I was a prosecutor, I always wanted to use proof of the accused's bad character, especially prior convictions. And the jury always wanted to know about prior convictions. The first question jurors asked me after a trial was, "Did he have a record?" Knowing about the defendant's criminal record would have made the jury's decision easier. It is precisely because it is easier to overlook the evidence in a case and rely on character evidence that jurors generally are not allowed to hear the prejudicial information.

By contrast, evidence of an animal's character is generally admissible. Perhaps animal habits are more uncomplicated and predictable than humans. For example, in animal complaint cases, I took testimony by uniformed animal control officers about Scruffy's *"modus operandi"* of digging out from under a fence or Spot's "propensity" to bite mail carriers. "Once a biter, always a biter" appears to be good law. Consequently, Judge Coyote was on firm legal ground when he took judicial notice of Rattlesnake's propensity to kill.

Of course, after the defendant's conviction, a judge needs character information in order to make a decision about the appropriate sentence. A judge must consider prior convictions. In modern courts, judges usually don't know the defendants who come before them for sentencing. They rely on written pre-sentence reports, recommendations of third parties, and letters and testimony from victims, family, and the community.

I remember an island judge who used his knowledge of the citizens in his jurisdiction to give creative sentences. When I was a new criminal deputy prosecutor, I was assigned to travel from court to court to prosecute traffic violations and minor crimes. For several months, I covered four courts on "the country club circuit," two in wealthy neighborhoods and two on islands.

Once a month, I took a ferry out to an island in the Puget Sound for the court session. One day, there was a simple assault case in which a young man, about nineteen years old, was charged with beating his parents. The judge heard the parents' testimony and pronounced the young man guilty. Just as Coyote knew Rattlesnake, this judge knew this young man. He did not give a typical sentence, such as one week in the county jail, a two hundred and fifty dollar fine, and two hundred and fifty hours of community service. He said, "I sentence you to stop drinking and stop hanging around with Billy Bob (or some such name). I further sentence you to get off the island and get a job." A plainspoken judge!

Why Owl Comes Out at Night

ॐ

(Burma)

Once, Owl lived like all the other birds. During the day, he hunted for food and visited with friends; he slept at night. One day, Owl was sitting on a branch when a bad boy aimed his slingshot at him. The boy hit Owl with a mud pellet that pierced into his rump. "Ouch," cried Owl and flew away to his friend Crow for help with his wound.

"Owl," said Crow. "I want to help you but I am no doctor. Let's go to Cuckoo. He is famous for his healing."

The two friends flew and found Cuckoo. He said, "I can help you, Owl, but you must pay for my services in advance." When Owl confessed that he had no money with him, Cuckoo refused to treat him. "How can I be sure you will pay me after you are well?"

Crow said, "I will be Owl's surety. If in the future, he does not pay, I will be good for the fee."

So Physician Cuckoo examined Owl. "There is a mud pellet in your rump. You need a water treatment; go sit in a shallow pool of water until the pain disappears."

Owl and Crow found a shallow pool and Owl soaked in the water for hours and hours. The mud pellet dissolved, the wound was cleansed, and the pain disappeared, just as Cuckoo had said. But Owl wasn't satisfied; he moped all the way home. He complained to his friend, "That was so easy. Just sit in water. I could have thought of that."

The next day, Cuckoo called on his patient. "Oh, Owl, I am so

pleased you are up and about. My water treatment must have worked."
Cuckoo was hinting for his fee.

But Owl said, "Do you call sitting in water a treatment?"

"Yes, indeed!" replied the physician. "I examined you. I diagnosed the problem. I prescribed a treatment, and you are recovered. Now
please give me my fee."

"You have earned no fee. Your 'treatment' was nothing but a
bath—which I do everyday anyway."

Cuckoo had foreseen that Owl would not pay when he got well.
Before he could say anything more, Owl drove Cuckoo from his house.
Cuckoo went straight to Crow to collect the debt. "Crow, you guaranteed
your friend would pay me. He refuses, so you must pay. That is the law."

Crow said, "Dr. Cuckoo, he must have been playing a joke on
you. Let's both go visit him." But Owl was nowhere to be found. They
called and called him, but he was gone.

"Well," said Cuckoo. "He cheated us both. But you still have to
pay."

"I haven't a penny in the whole wide world."

Cuckoo placed the matter before a judge. The judge ruled that
Crow had agreed to pay the debt. He said, "Crow, if you have no money,
you must work for Cuckoo. In the future, Crow, you must take care of
Cuckoo's eggs."

From that day to this day, Crow takes care of Cuckoo's eggs.
Crow never saw his friend Owl again, because Owl hid in a hollow tree
and only came out at night.

SOURCES:

- Maung Htin Aung gives two versions of this tale: a folktale and a
  Juristic tale. The folktale appears in "Why the Crow Looks After
  Cuckoo's Eggs." In *Selections from Burmese Folk Tales*. London: Oxford

University Press, 1951. The Justice tale is "The Cuckoo and the Crow." In *Burmese Law Tales: The Legal Element in Burmese Folk-lore*. London: Oxford University Press, 1962. In the Juristic tale, the Princess-Learned-in-the-Law upheld the point of law that a surety is liable for a debt when the debtor can not be found.

• Brockett, Eleanor. "The Crow, the Cuckoo and the Owl." In *Burmese and Thai Fairy Tales*. Chicago: Follett, 1965.

Whose Fault Was It?

❧

(Malaysia)

One day, Crocodile asked Mouse-deer, "Will you guard my eggs? I have ten fine eggs and I don't want to leave them unattended. I am going down to the river to catch a bite to eat."

"Yes," said Mouse-deer. "I will watch your eggs while you are gone."

"Thank you. I will soon be back to take charge of my precious eggs," said Crocodile as she crawled toward the river. Soon after she had gone, Woodpecker tapped out a War Dance alarm. When the alert sounded, Mouse-deer began the War Dance. Mouse-deer stood on his hind legs and kicked his forelegs high; he stood on his forelegs and kicked his hind legs high. While dancing his War Dance, Mouse-deer crushed Crocodile's eggs.

Crocodile returned, found her broken eggs, and complained to King Solomon. "Your Majesty, Mouse-deer has destroyed my eggs. Shouldn't he be punished?"

King Solomon replied, "I will make an inquiry into the matter of your broken eggs." Then he summoned Mouse-deer. "Did you break Crocodile's eggs?"

Mouse-deer answered, "Yes, your Majesty. Please pardon me; it was an accident. The War Dance alarm sounded, and it is my duty to dance the War Dance. I stepped on the eggs during the Dance. It is not my fault. It is Woodpecker's fault for tapping out the alarm."

King Solomon summoned Woodpecker. "Did you tap out the War Dance alarm that caused Mouse-deer to do the War Dance and break Crocodile's eggs?"

Woodpecker answered, "Yes, your Majesty. Please pardon me. I saw Lizard wearing his sword, and it is my duty to sound the alarm when there is danger. It is not my fault Crocodile's eggs were broken. It is Lizard's fault for putting on his sword."

King Solomon summoned Lizard. "Did you put on your sword that caused Woodpecker to tap out the War Dance alarm that caused Mouse-deer to do the War Dance and break Crocodile's eggs?"

Lizard answered, "Yes, your Majesty. Please pardon me. I saw Tortoise had put on his suit of armor, and it is my duty to put on my sword when there is danger. It is not my fault Crocodile's eggs were broken. It is Tortoise's fault for putting on his suit of armor."

King Solomon summoned Tortoise. "Did you put on your suit of armor, that caused Lizard to put on his sword that caused Woodpecker to tap out the War Dance alarm that caused Mouse-deer to do the War Dance and break Crocodile's eggs?"

Tortoise answered, "Yes, your Majesty. Please pardon me. I saw Crab sharpening his claws, and it is my duty to put on my suit of armor when there is danger. It is not my fault Crocodile's eggs were broken. It is Crab's fault for sharpening his claws."

King Solomon summoned Crab. "Did you sharpen your claws that caused Tortoise to put on his suit of armor that caused Lizard to put on his sword that caused Woodpecker to tap out the War Dance alarm that caused Mouse-deer to do the War Dance and break Crocodile's eggs?"

Crab answered, "Yes, your Majesty. Please pardon me. I saw Crocodile crawling towards the river to eat my little crab. It is my duty to sharpen my claws when my child is in danger. It is not my fault Crocodile's eggs were broken."

"No, Crab, it is not your fault," said King Solomon. "It is Crocodile's fault. She caused this chain of events that resulted in her eggs being broken. I sentence Crocodile to lay ten more eggs." So justice was done.

SOURCES:

- Tappan, Eva March. "Who Killed The Otter's Babies." In *The Children's Hour: Folk Stories and Fables*. Boston: Houghton Mifflin Company, 1907.
- Morris, James. "The Case of the Mouse-Deer and the Crocodile's Eggs." In *The Upstairs Donkey and Other Stolen Stories*. New York: Pantheon Books, 1961.
- Chang, Isabelle C. "The Sparrow and the Phoenix." In *Chinese Fairy Tales*. New York: Schocken Books, 1965. Mouse breaks Sparrow's eggs, which begins a chain of events that affects the lion and the phoenix eggs.
- Ausubel, Nathan, ed. "Whose Was the Blame." In *A Treasury of Jewish Folklore*. New York: Crown Publishers, 1948.

COMMENTS:

This story describes a chain of events reminiscent of such stories as "The House that Jack Built" or "The Gingerbread Man." This folktale also reflects reality because many accidents are chain events. For example, a one hundred-car pileup on a California freeway is a chain event that leads to the legal question of causation or "Whose Fault Was It?" The answer is fairly easy in this folktale because the animal who was damaged was the one who caused the chain of events; the chain was really a circle.

Negligence and Unforeseeable Plaintiffs

In my first weeks of law school, I studied about causation and legal responsibility in a famous case called *Palsgraf v Long Island R.R.*, 248 NY 339, 162 NE 99 (1928). It is perhaps the most well-known tort case among law students. I even knew about the case from a 1970s movie about law school, *The Paper Chase*. Palsgraf, an injured woman, sued the railroad and won. The railroad appealed, and the case was reviewed by a higher court of judges. The famous jurist Benjamin Cardoza wrote the opinion and set out the following facts:[1]

> Plaintiff [the person who was suing] was standing on a platform of defendant's railroad [the company which was sued after buying a ticket to go to Rockaway Beach.] A train stopped at the station, bound for another place. Two men ran forward to catch it. One of the men reached the platform of the car without mishap, though the train was already moving. The other man, carrying a package, jumped aboard the car, but seemed unsteady as if about to fall. A guard on the car, who held the door open, reached forward to help him in, and another guard on the platform pushed him from behind. In this act, the package was dislodged, and fell upon the rails. It was a package of small size, about fifteen inches long, and was covered by newspaper. In fact it contained fireworks, but there was nothing in appearance to give notice of its contents. The fireworks, when they fell, exploded. The shock of the explosion threw down some scales at the other end of the platform, many feet away. The scales struck the plaintiff, causing injuries for which she sues.[2]

When I first read these facts, I was reminded of an old silent movie about a slapstick chain of events. Then I began to think like a lawyer about "whose fault it was." The question was who had to pay for the plaintiff's injuries if there was a negligent breach of duty. Why wasn't the fireworks owner who ran for the moving train responsible? This man was never sued. Why? Perhaps he was never found or had no money. The railroad had the money or "the deep pocket."

A legal principle says that for there to be negligence, the injury must be foreseeable. If a reasonable person would not have foreseen any injury to anyone from the act, there is no duty owed to a person who is unexpectedly hurt. In the Palsgraf case, the act was the railroad employee pushing the man who was running from the train. It was foreseeable that the man who was pushed could have been injured. Therefore, if the man had been injured, the railroad would have been responsible for its negligence.

However, was the railroad responsible to this plaintiff, the woman bystander? There is a split in authority in this case. Cardoza and a majority of the appellate judges agreed that the railroad owed no duty to Palsgraf because it could not have foreseen that the guard's carelessness could injure her. The plaintiff was not in the zone of danger; the package did not appear hazardous. Therefore, the injured plaintiff got no money from the railroad company.

William Andrews, another judge on the court, disagreed and wrote a dissenting opinion. The "Andrew's view" said that a defendant could be responsible for the immediate and direct results of a careless act to an unforeseen person, "if he be outside what would generally be thought the danger zone." If a duty of care was owed to anyone, duty was owed to all. Therefore, the railroad would have been responsible for the plaintiff's injury.

The Palsgraf decision has been final for seventy years, but legal debates continue in law school classrooms and law reviews over "Whose fault was it?"

The Otters and the Fox

᭟

(India)

Two otters were fishing one day and had the good luck to catch a huge fish. The fish made a valiant struggle and was about to break free. One otter jumped in the river to throw the fish on the bank. The fish was so strong that it pulled the otter along the current. The second otter dived in to help, and together they landed the fish on the bank. Both otters were exhausted.

When they were recovered from their struggle, the otters began to quarrel about dividing their catch. Each claimed the greater share, and neither wanted the head or tail.

Along came a fox, who stopped to listen to their dispute. The otters turned to him.

"I jumped into the water to save this fish," the first otter explained. "I should have the greater share. Don't you agree?"

"Wrong," argued the second otter. "You and the fish would have been swept away in the current if I had not saved you both. I deserve a bigger share. Tell us who is right."

The fox said gravely, "I have judged many cases like this. Here is my decision." The fox cut the fish in three parts. "This is your share," said fox as he gave the first otter the head of the fish. "This is your share," said fox as he gave the second otter the tail.

"But what of the body of the fish?" asked the otters.

"That is my share for acting as judge," said the fox as he ran off with most of the fish in his mouth.

When the fox arrived home, his wife exclaimed admiringly, "Husband, what a clever fisherman you are! How did you catch so great a fish?"

"I caught him without having to go near the water," replied her husband. "I met two otters who knew how to catch the fish together, but they did not know how to agree together when it came time to divide it. And their quarrel made me a better fisherman than either of them. Fighting leads to losses."

SOURCES:

- Gaer, Joseph. "The Otters and the Fox." In The *Fables of India* Boston, Toronto: Little, Brown and Co., 1955.

- Reed, Gwendolyn. "How to Catch a Fish." *The Talkative Beasts: Myths, Fables and Poems of India*. New York: Lothrop, Lee and Shepard, 1969.

- De Roin, Nancy. "Decide for Yourself." In *Jataka Tales*. Boston: Houghton Mifflin, 1975.

- Htin Aung, Maung, and Helen G. Trager. "Partnership." In *A Kingdom Lost for a Drop of Honey*. New York: Parents' Magazine Press, 1968. In a dispute between Otter and Jackal, Judge Rabbit makes a fair division by cutting the fish down the center so both get the same portion of the head, tail, and belly.

- Nahmad, H. M. "The Ape and Two Cats." In *The Peasant and the Donkey*. New York: Henry Z. Walck, 1968. An ape acts as the judge to divide a piece of cheese, and eats all the cheese. .

- Lee, F. Hied. "Dividing the Cheese." In *Folktales of all Nations*. New York: Tudor Publishing, 1930. A monkey divides rice cakes for two cats and nibbles on both until they are even.

COMMENTS:

This story is one of the Jataka tales, also called Buddhist Birth-Stories, which tell of Buddha in his former existences. Many are in the form of fables, each representing an episode in the life of the Bodisat, as Buddha is called before his enlightenment.

On first reading of this Jakata tale, I thought, "It is just a clever, trickster tale, similar to the ape and the two cats story." Then I read Htin's Burmese version with the even division and thought, "Surely this ending must be the true Jakata tale because it teaches fairness." After I discovered two more versions that had the judge taking the biggest share, I reflected that the lesson might be that "Fighting leads to losses." Every student knows that going to the principal to settle a dispute means more trouble; likewise, every employee knows that going to the boss means more difficulty.

Working as an attorney, I observed that people involved in court battles, both civil and criminal, were seldom satisfied with the results. Even if people won, they complained about time wasted, emotional strain, unfair treatment by the legal system, and so on. The following passages echo the moral of this Jakata tale: it is better to settle disagreements.

Even-Handed Justice
BY NICHOLAS BOILEAU*

Once, says an author, where I need not say,
Two travellers found an oyster on their way.
Both fierce, both hungry, the dispute grew strong,
When scale in hand, Dame Justice passed along.
Before her each with clamor pleads the laws,
Explains the matter, and would win the cause.

---

* Boileau was a seventeenth-century artist.

Dame Justice, weighing long the doubtful right,
Takes, opens, swallows it before their sight.
The cause of strife removed so rarely well,
"There, take," says Justice, "take you each a shell,
We thrive in courthouses on fools like you.
'Twas a fat oyster; live in peace–Adieu."

LITIGATION: A machine which you go into as a pig and come out as a sausage.

— Ambrose Bierce
Between 1881 and 1906, Bierce published his
definitions in newspapers and *The Cynic's Word Book.*

Avoid Litigation

When Abraham Lincoln was a lawyer in Illinois, he tried to encourage settling disputes without litigation. According to legend, when two farmers went to Lincoln over a boundary dispute, they were encouraged to come to an agreement without going to court. He told them, "Now, if you go on with this, it will cost both of your farms, and will entail an enmity that will last for generations and perhaps lead to murder. Now, I want you two to sit down in my office while I am gone to dinner and talk it over, and try to settle it. And, to secure you from any interruption, I will lock the door." By the time Mr. Lincoln returned to release the men, the matter was settled.[1]

Lincoln also told his legal colleagues, "Discourage litigation. Persuade your neighbors to compromise whenever you can. ... As a peacemaker, the lawyer has a superior opportunity of being a good man. There will still be business enough."

Coyote and Horned Toad

⋘

(Navajo)

One day Coyote was very hungry. He knew Horned Toad had a big cornfield. Coyote went to Horned Toad's cornfield, stole some green corn, and ate it.

When Horned Toad saw Coyote, he called, "Coyote, this is my corn. I worked hard to grow it. I like people to ask my permission to eat my corn."

"Will you share some corn?" asked Coyote.

"Yes," said Horned Toad. And he cooked green corn for Coyote. Coyote ate the corn.

"I am still hungry," said Coyote. Horned Toad cooked more corn. Coyote ate. "Give me more," said Coyote. Horned Toad cooked corn again. Coyote ate again.

"More!" demanded Coyote a fourth time.

Horned Toad said, "No more. I am tired of your begging. Plant your own garden."

"If you do not feed me, I will eat you," threatened Coyote.

Horned Toad began to swell in size. "Do not eat me or you will be sorry," said Toad.

"I will not be sorry. A big toad will make a good meal." And Coyote swallowed Horned Toad in one gulp. "Now I feel full," said Coyote as he lay down to take a nap. "I will keep Toad's hogan* and the cornfield for my own."

---

* A Navajo house, built of earthen wall supported by timber.

While Coyote slept, Horned Toad got his strength back. He began to stir in Coyote's stomach. "Ouch," said Coyote in his sleep, "the green corn is giving me a stomachache."

But it was not the green corn that was causing Coyote's pain, it was Horned Toad. He made a loud hissing noise that woke Coyote. "What's that noise?" asked Coyote.

"Hsss! It is me," Horned Toad laughed. "I said you would be sorry if you swallowed me." Horned Toad walked around and scraped his long pointed spikes into Coyote.

"You are hurting my stomach. Get out!" Coyote commanded.

Horned Toad walked and swelled and scraped.

"You are hurting my liver. Get out!" Coyote demanded.

Horned Toad walked and swelled and scraped.

"You are hurting my lungs. Get out!" Coyote pleaded.

Horned Toad walked and swelled and scraped.

"You are hurting my heart. Get out!" Coyote begged.

When Coyote fell dead, Horned Toad got out.

But Coyote did not stay dead. He kept his vital life force in the tip of his nose and the tip of his tail. Coyote soon came to life again and looked around for more mischief.

SOURCES:

- Hogner, Dorothy Childs. "Coyote and Horned Toad." In *Navajo Winter Nights*. New York: E. M. Hale and Company, 1938.
- Link, Margaret Schevill. "The Changing Coyote" In *The Pollen Path: A Collection of Navajo Myths*. Stanford, Calif.: Stanford University Press, 1956.
- Morgan, William. "Coyote and Horned Toad." In *Navajo Coyote Tales*. Santa Fe: Ancient City Press, 1988.

COMMENTS:

Not all justice is the result of a formal legal proceeding; some justice is the result of natural consequences. If you swallow a horned toad, the natural consequence will be punishment enough.

The preceding tale about the otters and the anecdote about Abraham Lincoln both made good arguments for avoiding litigation and settling disputes among the disputing parties. But this tale about Coyote and Horned Toad illustrates that when one of the parties is bigger or unprincipled, like Coyote, the weaker party can "get eaten alive."

Attorneys and courts are effective when there is inequity between the parties, such as when a consumer sues a big corporation. But when the disputants are peers, mediation can be effective. The Navajo Peacemaker Court is one example of how parties can get outside help to mediate disputes.

Navajo Peacemaker Court

The Navajo Nation has two types of dispute resolution: the predominant Navajo Nation courts, which use the Anglo-American justice system, and the new Navajo Peacemaker Court, which uses tribal custom and tradition.[1] The modern Navajo Nation courts developed as a result of the changes forced on the Navajo; by contrast, the traditional ways of the Peacemaker court survived in spite of these changes.

The Navajo call themselves the *diné*, "the people;" the word Navajo is Spanish. Their homelands in the Southwest were annexed by the United States in 1848. The United States acquired the region because of its victory in the Mexican War. In an effort to dominate the region, federal troops conducted campaigns into Navajo territory to subdue Navajo raids on ranchers' livestock.[2] Eventually, 8,500 Navajo were forced on "The Long Walk" to Bosque Redondo and Fort Sumner in

New Mexico.[3]

In 1868, a United States treaty created a Navajo reservation in New Mexico, Arizona, and Utah. The 3.5 million acres allotted were about one-tenth of their former homelands.[4] The Navajo were allowed to go to the reservation and were supervised by the Bureau of Indian Affairs.

In 1892, the federal government created a court system called the Courts of Indian Offenses. The Navajo judges were appointed by federal officials, the law was United States law rather than customary tribal law, the rules were written by the Commissioner of Indian Affairs, and the decisions were reviewed by government agents.[5] These courts were very unlike the Navajo way of resolving disputes. However, the judges continued to refer disputes to the community leaders to be mediated in the Navajo way. These referrals were done informally, and the mediations took place outside the government legal system.[6]

The Navajo Nation Tribal Council gradually assumed more responsibly for self-governing. In 1959, the modern Navajo Nation court system was established by the Tribal Council. The system, which is based on United States law, has seven district courts, five family courts, and a court of appeals located throughout the reservation. These courts handle criminal cases, contract disputes, probate, divorces, and all the legal matters found in a United States court.[7]

The Honorable Robert Yazzie, Chief Justice of the Navajo nation, describes these courts as using the Anglo-American "vertical" system of justice. The judges are at the top in the hierarchy of power and make the decisions. The parties in the dispute have limited power in the legal process. They are considered adversaries; someone wins and someone loses. Punishing the offender is often more important than compensating the victim.[8]

In 1982, the Judicial Conference of the Navajo Nation formed the Navajo Peacemaker Court as an experimental alternative to

Anglo-American style litigation. The roles adopted by judges are consistent with the traditional methods that had been used continually, though not officially, up until that time.[9] The district courts provide support for the Peacemaker courts by referring cases, keeping records, and enforcing decisions made through mediation. The new Peacemaker Court is thus a blend of the old and the new. The Navajo Peacemaker Court Manual lists some types of disputes that would be appropriate for mediation: family disputes, neighbor problems such as animal trespass, alcohol problems among family and neighbors, and other personal disagreements.[10]

Judge Yazzie describes the Peacemaker Court as an example of a "horizontal" (or circular) justice system which uses local mediation. The circle is an appropriate symbol for the court because it represents people gathered for discussion.[11] There are no rules of evidence or other procedural matters that rule formal litigation. Attorneys may not represent parties.[12]

The parties who select the Peacemaker Court, or the district court judge, choose an elder, community leader, or religious leader to be the peacemaker (naat'aanii). The duties of the peacemaker are to assemble the parties and their families, to guide the discussion between the parties, and to coordinate activities with the district courts.[13] The peacemaker might speak about Navajo values, give advice, or offer a prayer. Without using coercion, the peacemaker attempts to lead the group to a solution that will help the victim, be agreed upon by all parties, and restore harmony in the relationships. The object of the Peacemaker Court is to solve problems, rather than determine who is right or wrong.

The parties and their families come together in a relaxed atmosphere. Everyone in the dispute speaks, even the family members. If a solution is reached that is acceptable to the parties, the results may be written down and signed by a judge. If the dispute has not been resolved, the parties can litigate in the Navajo Nation courts.[14]

Though there are no official statistics about the effectiveness of the new Peacemaker Court, in 1991 one peacemaker, Freddy Lee, estimated that eighty percent of the sessions were effectively settled.[15] Michael D. Lieder, in his article, "Navajo Dispute Resolution and Promissory Obligations," says that the process is less effective when an outsider causes an injury; an outsider may lack the feeling of responsibility to the community which is necessary to reach consensus.[16]

Whose Children?

✵

(Africa)

One day, on the plains of an African savannah, a mother ostrich was taking her chicks for a walk. Her children stopped to peck at bugs and seeds. The ostrich spread her wings to give them shade. She sang a little song to urge them along:

Sweet, fat children
Follow me.
Sweet, fat babies
Follow me.

Nearby, under the shade of a tree, lay a young lion. He had feasted all night and was napping, belly to the sun. His ears twitched at the sound of the ostrich's song, and his half-closed eyes opened. He rolled over, yawned, and focused on the six chicks bouncing through the tall grass. His muscles tightened into a crouch; he began to silently slink toward the ostrich family.

Mother Ostrich was extremely wary and turned her head on her long neck to scan for any dangers. At first, she did not see the lion who blended so well with the brown grass, but when she detected a movement, she set up a cry:

Run and hide, children!
Run and hide!

Mother Ostrich began to run, not to escape from the lion, but to lead him away from her precious chicks. She beat her wings; she ran in zig-zag; she called out. But the lazy lion had no intention of chasing the fast bird who had a vicious kick. It was just too hot! Besides, those chicks were his just for the rounding up.

Lion easily herded the ostrich chicks and led them back to the tree. He held his tail as high as a flag and sang:

> *Sweet, fat children*
> *Follow me.*
> *Sweet, fat babies*
> *Follow me.*

Mother Ostrich put out a distress call when she saw her children following Lion.

> *Lion stole my children. Help! Help!*
> *Lion stole my children. Help! Help!*

Lion settled in the shade with the chicks huddled between his large paws. He watched and waited to see what would happen next. Ostrich continued to call:

> *Lion stole my children. Help! Help!*
> *Lion stole my children. Help! Help!*

Animals began to gather. Wildebeest, Gazelle, Wart Hog, Hyena, and Mongoose came. The animals moved as close as they dared and came to rest beside a tall termite nest. Ostrich was pacing and shaking her feathers.

"Give me back my chicks!" demanded Ostrich to Lion.

"What chicks?" asked Lion innocently.

"My chicks—under your very nose!" she replied.

"These are not your chicks; these are my newborn cubs," said Lion. "Let the animals judge this dispute." Lion addressed the animals. "Jury, whose children are these?"

The animals milled around in confusion and fear in the presence of their enemy. Wildebeest said, "I will preside: I am the largest." He climbed on top of the termite nest. "Who will speak?" No one spoke. Wildebeest singled out Gazelle. "Whose children are these?"

Gazelle spoke timidly, "I am not entirely sure. But I see the babies have two feet like Ostrich. Lion has four feet."

Lion growled, and Gazelle stepped back. "My children have four feet." He indicated the wings of the babies. "See! Their feet are still growing." Then Lion got up and paced back and forth. The chicks followed. "See how they follow me. Children follow their parents."

"Yes," said Gazelle. "Children follow their parents. They are Lion's cubs."

Ostrich hissed.

"Wart Hog," said Wildebeest. "Whose children are these?"

Wart Hog spoke nervously, "I am not entirely sure. But I see the babies have long necks like Ostrich."

Lion bared his long teeth. "Of course, my children have long necks; they are still growing. Soon they will have thick, strong necks like mine, covered with manes. Look at their big eyes and long eyelashes, just like mine."

"Yes," said Wart Hog. "The children have big eyes and long eyelashes like Lion. They are Lion's cubs."

Ostrich hissed and snorted.

"Hyena," said Wildebeest. "Whose children are these?" Hyena shrank and cowered. "I am not entirely sure. But I see the children have two toes like Ostrich."

Lion whipped his long tail. "My children have five toes on each foot; they are still growing. Look at their spots. They are spotted and dabbled, just like lion cubs."

"Yes," said Hyena. "They are spotted. They are Lion's cubs."

Ostrich hissed, snorted, and squealed.

So it continued. Every animal agreed with every reason Lion gave for why the chicks belonged to him. Finally, Wildebeest asked Mongoose, "Whose children are these?"

Mongoose moved closer to the termite nest. He turned and addressed the council: "Stupid you are. Afraid you are. When are feathers begot by fur?"

Then Mongoose spoke to Lion, "They are Ostrich's chicks. Let them go." Lion charged Mongoose, but Mongoose was swift and slim. Mongoose dived into one of the holes in the termite nest. The animals scattered across the plains as Lion roared and dug at the termite mound. Mongoose escaped unseen through a tunnel on the other side. During the hubbub, Ostrich quietly gathered up her chicks and led them to safety:

Sweet, fat children
Follow me.
Sweet, fat babies
Follow me.

SOURCES:

- Hollis, Alfred C. "The Story of the Ostrich Chicks." In *The Masai, Their Language and Folklore.* Oxford: The Clarendon Press, 1905.
- Bryan, Ashley. "Lion and the Ostrich Chicks." In *Lion and the Ostrich Chicks and Other African Folk Tales.* New York: Atheneum, 1986. Retold from Hollis.
- Aardema, Verna. "The Lonely Lioness and the Ostrich Chicks." In *Tales for the Third Ear from Equatorial Africa.* New York: E. P. Dutton and Co., Inc.
- Heady, Eleanor. "The Lion and the Ostrich Chicks." In *Jambo, Sungura: Tales from East Africa.* New York: W. W. Norton and Co., 1965.

The Bell of Atri

(Italy)

Long ago, there was a town in Italy called Atri. Because the people desired harmony and justice, they hung a large bell in the center of the town. The people said, "Anyone who has been wronged can ring the bell. We will all gather and settle the dispute."

Years passed, and no one rang the bell. Perhaps just seeing the bell in the square caused the citizens to deal fairly with each other. The rope of the bell hung to the ground; over time, a grape vine twined around it.

During those years, a knight returned to Atri from foreign wars. He rode into town on his strong and beautiful horse. He told everyone of the battles. "The only reason I am alive is because this swift steed carried me safely out of danger. I will be grateful all of her days," he told the people.

The knight returned to his farm and put away his sword and armor. He put his beloved horse in a warm stall. "I promise you, my brave friend, you will always have a bed and a bucket of oats." But the horse had been exhausted and chilled in the battles and began to decline in health. At first, the knight took tender care of his animal.

Slowly, the knight forgot about his battles; he became just a busy farmer tending his stock and tilling the soil. The once brave and beautiful horse was now deaf and blind. "You eat too much and you take up too much space," the master said. Finally, one day, he said, "You are useless."

He felt justified in taking the old horse out of the stable, taking off her bridle, and driving her off with a stick.

The old horse was confused. She stood outside the gate with her head hung down. Night fell and the wind and snow came. The horse began to stumble around to find shelter and food. In her blind search, she walked toward town. By dawn, the horse was standing in the village square. She chanced upon the rope of bell which hung to the ground. She began to nibble on the vine encircling the rope. The bell began to ring.

The people poured into the street. "Who calls for justice?" they asked. Everyone knew the knight's horse. They saw her; thin, blind and covered with snow. But they remembered her hour of glory when her master had promised gratitude. "She has a right to ring the bell and demand justice," the people agreed.

The knight was called before the town to explain his cruel behavior; he had no explanation. He was ordered to take care of his horse and treat her with loving kindness for all of her days. The faithful horse was led home to a warm stall and a bucket of oats.

SOURCES:

- Baldwin, James. "The Bell of Atri." In *Favorite Tales of Long Ago*. New York: E. P. Dutton and Co., Inc., 1955.

- Harrell, John, and Mary Harrell. "The Bell of Atri." In *A Storyteller's Treasury*. Berkeley, Calif.: Harrell Publishing, 1977.

- Carey, Bonnie. "Catch-the-Wind." In *Baba Yaga's Geese and Other Russian Stories*. Bloomington, Ind.: Indiana University Press, 1973.

- Komroff, Manuel. "Story of the Bell of Justice." In *The Great Fables*. New York: Tudor Publishing Co., 1935. In this fouteenth-century Roman fable, a serpent rings the bell of justice when a toad takes possession of her nest. The blind emperor evicts the toad, and is given a precious gem by the grateful serpent. The gem heals the emperor's blindness.

- Aesop. *Aesop's Fables*. Trans. V .S. Vernon Jones. New York: Garden City Publishing Co., 1939.

Also Roche, Paul. *New Tales from Aesop*. Notre Dame, Ind.: University of Notre Dame Press, 1982.

COMMENTS:

Anti-cruelty Laws

The United States was the first county to enact laws to protect animals from cruel treatment. In 1641, the Puritans voted on their legal code, "The Body of Liberties," which contained one hundred liberties to be observed. Liberty 92 declared that cruelty to animals was forbidden: "No man shall exercise any Tirranny or Crueltie towards any bruite Creature which are usuallie kept for man's use."[1] Currently, all fifty states have anti-cruelty laws that generally say that animals have the right to:

- Food, water and shelter.
- Protection from cruel treatment.
- Protection from abandonment.
- Protection from poisoning.[2]

Animal Protection Societies

Although there are laws to protect animals, as a nation, we abandon thousands of animals each year. As a result, there are groups that maintain shelters for unwanted animals and investigate reports of animal mistreatment. In 1866, the first anti-cruelty society was founded by Henry Bergh. The American Society for the Prevention of Cruelty to Animals (ASPCA) became the model for about one thousand local societies in the

United States. For example, storyteller Pat Peterson is a member of the Cascade Animal Protection Society. She rescues abandoned cats, takes them for medical treatment, and gives them foster care until they are placed with a family. She is still fostering a handsome white cat, Buddy, who I found injured and hungry in the traffic in front of my condo in Seattle.

Animal Rights

Our national attitudes towards animals have changed significantly since the Pilgrims arrived and we began the expansion into the West. We no longer condone the slaughter of bison and wildlife, for example. Animal rights debates remain, however, extremely divisive. Common conflicting opinions include:

- Animals should not be used for experiments because it is inhumane, inadequately regulated and is of no benefit **vs.** animal experimentation is necessary to benefit human health.

- Modern farming and methods of slaughter are inhumane **vs.** farmers provide good nutrition, medical care, and shelter for their animals in order to raise healthy stock.

- Meat is a tasty, nutritious essential in human diet **vs.** meat is an unnecessary food that is full of fat and added chemicals, and rain forests are burned and water supplies depleted to raise cattle.

- Zoos are educational and help save endangered species **vs.** zoos are a cruel captivity of wild animals and produce inbred animals.

- Endangered species must be protected by changing the way humans fish, hunt, and develop the land **vs.** human economic growth and development take precedence over the extinction of a few species.

- Hunting is a cruel and unnecessary sport in modern society **vs.** hunting is a regulated activity which thins overpopulated species and provides meat to families.

The question at the heart of these debates is whether animals have rights. Should animals have the same rights as people? Do some animals have more rights than other animals? Should humans change the way they live to accommodate animal rights? These questions will be asked again and again as we continue to share a crowded planet.[3]

ॐ *Three* ॐ

SOME ARE WISE; SOME ARE OTHERWISE

Trickster tales are found in folktales from every culture. Perhaps it is because a moral lesson can be learned from a laugh as well as a lecture. Some of the stories in this chapter are about famous, or perhaps infamous, rogues: Anansi the Spider from Jamaica, John from the American South, and Coyote from the Navajo Nation. Other tricksters are nameless: the Irish lawyer who battles the Devil for her mother's soul; the Danish lawyer who advises his client to act crazy in court.

Some of the tricksters are successful in their tricks, such as the Hodja foiling a burglar, or John outwitting the plantation owner. Others, like the boy who wanted to be a robber, are "hoisted on their own petard" and out-tricked. In other words, some are wise, and some are otherwise. But all have been remembered through the years for their wit, boldness, and spunk.

A Bargain is a Bargain

(Ireland)

There once was a poor widow woman, and she had three children: two sons and a daughter. They were her every joy. Clever children they were, and she wanted to give them the best schooling, so they could make something of themselves. Since the widow had no money, no jewels, no property, she sold the only thing she had—her immortal soul. And of course, she sold it to the Devil. It was that much she loved those babes.

The Devil gave her a bag of gold sovereigns and said, "I'll be back for you in twenty years." Then he settled back until the time he could collect on his debt. He watched and waited and he watched and waited as the widow spent every coin on education. A good investment it was. The children studied hard and made her proud. The oldest son became a priest; the second son a doctor; and the daughter became a lawyer. As the years went by the widow became old and ill.

When the twenty years had passed, the widow lay dying. Her son the priest was at her bedside praying. There was a rumble of thunder, a crash of lightning. The door flung open, and in walked the Devil. The priest blocked the way, but the Devil pushed him aside. "Out of me way, I've come for your mother." The priest fell to his knees and prayed that his mother be spared. The Devil gave her one more year of life. Why did the Devil grant an extra year? Perhaps he wanted to court the soul of the priest.

When that year was up, the widow again lay dying. Her son the doctor was at her bedside. There was a rumble of thunder, a clap of lightning, and the door flung open. In walked the Devil. The doctor blocked the way. "Out of me way, I've come for your mother." The doctor fell to his knees and pleaded that his mother be spared. And he got one more year off the Devil. Maybe the Devil had a tender spot for moms.

When that year was up, the widow lay dying. There was a rumble of thunder, a clap of lightning. The door flung open and the Devil came a third time to claim the old woman. He found the daughter there. The Devil called out, "Don't be using any woman's tears on me. I'm here to take my due. A bargain is a bargain." But the daughter did not weep.

Then the Devil remembered she was a lawyer. "And don't be using your legal words and your courtroom tricks on me."

She said, "You've given sparing to my mother twice already, and I know you can't be expected to do it again."

"What a fair-minded lawyer," thought the Devil.

"But," says she, "my brothers have not kissed our mother farewell. They will be here soon. Please, just a few more minutes. Will you give her sparing till—till that stub of a candle burns away?"

The Devil turned and looked at the candle burning on the table. It was only a stub of candle, soon to sputter and die.

"All right," said the Devil. "Until the candle burns away—not a second more."

"A bargain is a bargain," the lawyer said. Before the Devil knew what was happening, she walked to the table, picked up the candle and blew it out! And then she put it in her pocket.

That was that! It was clear the candle would never be relit, and would never burn away. The Devil left without the mother's soul.

SOURCES:

- Shannon, George. "The Lawyer and the Devil." In *More Stories to Solve: Fifteen Folktales from Around the World.* New York: Greenwillow Books, 1990. The tale is told in riddle form.

- Williamson, Duncan. *May the Devil Walk Behind Me: Scottish Traveler Tales.* Edinburgh: Connongate Publishing Ltd., 1989.

- Yolen, Jane. "The Lawyer and the Devil." In *Favorite Folktales from Around the World.* New York: Pantheon Books, 1986. From Michael J. Murphy, *Now You're Talking ... Folk Tales from the North of Ireland.* Belfast: Blackstaff Press, 1975.

- Briggs, Katherine. "The Candle." In *A Dictionary of British Folk-Tales in the English Language.* Bloomington, Ind.: Indiana University Press, 1970. V. 1. An old woman saves a pretty maid from the Devil with the candle trick.

- Giddings, Ruth Warner. "The Yaqui Doctor." In *Yaqui Myths and Legends.* Tucson, Ariz.: The University of Arizona Press, 1959. In this Native American story from Arizona, Death is the Godfather who is tricked by the candle being blown out.

COMMENTS:

I changed the gender of the lawyer from male to female because there are no women lawyers in traditional folktales. I wanted a character with whom modern women attorneys could identify.

The lawyer tricks the devil in this story with her canny knowledge of contract law. When Kellye Teste, a contracts professor at Seattle University School of Law, heard this story, she said, "That's a great story." She explained that the lawyer and the Devil made a bargain that he would forebear taking the mother's soul until the candle burned away. The burning of the candle was a "condition precedent," or something that had to happen first. But the lawyer prevented the occurrence of the condition precedent by blowing out the candle. She broke the terms of the bargain; if the Devil had known contract law, he could have snatched the soul and ran. Instead, he thought a bargain was a bargain!

The Devil and Daniel Webster

There is another story about a lawyer beating the Devil: "The Devil and Daniel Webster" written by Stephen Vincent Benet in 1937. The lawyer is the historic figure, Daniel Webster, born on a farm in New Hampshire in 1782. After studying at Dartmouth College, he was admitted to the bar. Webster argued two hundred and forty-nine cases before the U.S. Supreme Court, including *McCulloch v Maryland,* which determined the distribution of powers between the federal government and the states. He was a fierce defender of the Union and a strong national government. He had a large head, deep dark eyes, and a thunderous voice that gave him hypnotic power when he spoke. His trial and oratorical skills made him a national hero.

In "The Devil and Daniel Webster," a New Hampshire farmer, Jabez Stone, sold his soul to the Devil in order to prosper. When the Devil came to collect after seven years, the farmer asked Webster to defend him at trial. The jury box was filled with American villains that the Devil brought from Hell; the judge was John Hawthorne, the cruel Puritan fanatic who presided over the investigations of witchcraft in Salem, Massachusetts. But Webster softened their flinty hearts with his sweet words; he told the story of the early days of America, and the dreams and struggles of ordinary men like the farmer, Jabez Stone. In Steven Benet's account, Webster's "voice could search the heart, and that was his gift and strength." The jury found for Jabez Stone and said, "Perhaps 'tis not strictly in accordance with the evidence, but even the damned may salute the eloquence of Mr. Webster."[1]

General Moulton and the Devil

∽

(Colonial America)

Jonathan Moulton of Hampton, New Hampshire, had been a general in the colonial wars. But his neighbors did not trust him, for he loved money above all else. And he schemed to be the wealthiest man in the province.

One dark night, just after the wars, the general sat musing at his fireside. "If only I could have gold enough," he muttered, "I'd sell my soul."

The fire exploded as something came down the chimney. The general was startled as a man stepped from a shower of sparks. The tall visitor was clad in black leather, white ruffles, and jeweled buttons; he was unsinged by the flames.

"Let's get down to business," said the elegant stranger. "In fifteen minutes, I must be fifteen miles away." Picking up a live coal in his fingers, he looked at his pocket watch. "Is it a bargain?"

"What bargain?" replied Jonathan, who was still stunned by the unusual arrival of his visitor.

"General, don't be coy. The bargain is: in exchange for your soul, I will make you the richest man in the province. Sign my contract, and on the first day of every month, I will fill your boots with gold."

Jonathan hesitated. "What proof is there that you can do your part of the bargain?" The visitor ran his fingers through his hair and a shower of gold guineas jingled to the floor. They were glowing hot, but the general fell on hands and knees and gathered them up.

"Sign!"

Still Jonathan hesitated. "Give me a minute to consider."

"You have wasted my time with your idle musing," scoffed the stranger, and he reached to take back the coins. But Jonathan could not bear to give up the coins in his hands or the gold in his dreams.

"First, let us have a drink," stalled Jonathan, as he filled two cups with rum. The stranger lit his rum with a burning coal and raised his cup in a salute. "To our bargain," he called and gulped down the flaming brew. Then holding out a parchment scroll and a plumed pen, the stranger commanded, "Sign."

Jonathan swigged a mouthful of rum to moisten his dry mouth before reaching a trembling hand out for the paper. The scroll unrolled and Jonathan saw a row of signatures—some of the most prestigious people in the region had already sealed bargains. "Well, I am in good company," said Jonathan as he took the pen and wrote "General Jonathan Moulton of Hampton."

"Done!" cried the visitor and stepped into the fireplace. Then he paused and looked Jonathan in the eye. "I give you this warning, my crafty friend: keep this bargain fairly, or you will regret it." The fire flared, and the stranger vanished.

On the last night of the month, Jonathan hung his boots in the fireplace and ran down the next morning to find them filled with gold coins. Each month, the general grew richer and richer, but not fast enough to suit him. He went into town and bought the biggest hip boots he could find and placed them in the fireplace. The next morning the hip boots brimmed with coins. Still unsatisfied, Jonathan continued to scheme for more money.

Then one night the visitor stood on the roof to make his monthly payment. Pouring guineas down the chimney, he emptied bushel after bushel of gold. He peered down; the boots were not full. He finally climbed down the fireplace to investigate. The hip boots were hanging on the grate with the soles cut away. The floor beneath the boots was also cut away. The cellar was knee-deep in coins. The visitor smiled and vanished.

A few minutes later, the general woke to the smell of sulfur and the sound of crackling flames. He escaped in his nightshirt and stood on the lawn with his neighbors to watch the fire consume his house. No one tried to stop the fire, perhaps because the fire was too hot, perhaps because the general was a miser who deserved his fate. At first, Jonathan cried out, pulled his hair, and tried to rush back into the house; however, the thought that gold would melt but not burn restrained him. Before the embers were cool, he was rummaging in the remains. The gold was gone.

Soon after, the general was found dead. The town gave him a decent funeral for the sake of his war record. The day after the funeral, his coffin was found, dug up, and flung open. It was empty.

SOURCES:

• Skinner, Charles M. "General Moulton and the Devil." In *Myths and Legends of Our Own Land. Vol. 2.* Philadelphia: J. B. Lippincott, 1896. Reissued Detroit: Singing Tree Press, Book Tower, 1969.
• Dorson, Richard. "Supernatural Stories." In *Jonathan Draws the Long Bow: New England Popular Tales and Legends.* Cambridge, Mass.: Harvard University Press, 1946.
• Taft, Lewis. "General Moulton's Boot." In *Profile of Old New England: Yankee Legends, Tales and Folk-lore.* New York: Dodd, Mead and Co., 1965.
• Raskin, Joseph and Edith Raskin. "Jonathan Moulton and the Devil." In *Tales Our Settlers Told.* New York: Lothrop, Lee and Shepard, 1971.

COMMENTS:

The story of Jonathan Moulton is a legend: a story based on a factual event which has been repeated over time so that the facts have become fictionalized. In all versions, the Moulton legend has a central theme of a miserly general with unexplained wealth and a house that burnt down. But accounts vary about the demise of Moulton. Some say he died when he rushed into the fire to save his gold. Some say that he was seen leaving the ashes in the company of a man in black. A local woman reported that she saw the Devil flying off with the soul of Moulton.[1]

Salem Witch Trials

General Moulton lived in a dangerous time and place to have his neighbors thinking that he was in league with the Devil. Belief in the Devil and witchcraft was commonplace in colonial America. The infamous Cotton Mather preached in one of his sermons, "The meeting-house, wherein we assemble for the worship of God, is filled with many holy people...; but if our eyes were so refined as the servant of the prophet had his of old, I suppose we should now see a throng of devils in this very place."[2] Mather's fiery sermons contributed to the hysteria which resulted in nineteen executions for witchcraft in Salem, Massachusetts.

In 1692, at the beginning of the Salem Witch Trials, Massachusetts was in political and legal upheaval. It had been an autonomous colony, but lost its charter from England.

During the winter of 1691-92, Tituba, a servant from the West Indies, read fortunes and taught magic to a group of young girls. The girls, aged nine to twenty, later fell into trances, had visions, and made odd noises. They were declared victims of maleficia, malicious acts caused by

witches. When urged by a minister and doctor, the girls said they were
bewitched by Tituba and two other women.

The first public inquest was held in a church and led by two magistrates with no legal training: John Hawthorne and Jonathan Corwin. The
magistrates did not conduct an impartial investigation; rather, they
accused three women of witchcraft: Tituba, the servant, Sarah Goode, a
poor, pregnant woman, and Sarah Osburn, an old woman dragged from
her sick bed. When the women denied making contracts with the Devil
and tormenting the girls, the girls fell into fits before the gathered villagers. They claimed to see visions or specters that no one else could see.
Tituba gave testimony against the other women. She reported riding on
sticks with Goode and Osburn behind her.[3] The girls' accusations
expanded to include two hundred people, and by May the jails were full of
people awaiting trial. At the same time, Massachusetts went through a
change: England made it a royal province and appointed a new governor.
A special court was appointed for the witchcraft trials.[4]

The trials commenced, and neighbors began testifying against
neighbors. Most of the testimony was "spectral evidence" or visions of
evil deeds. The girls were in attendance, having fits when anyone denied
guilt. The people who confessed to witchcraft were held in prison and
never brought to the gallows. Those who maintained their innocence
were quickly hanged. Some of the accused included:

- George Burrough, a former pastor of Salem Village. One of the girls
  said that his two dead wives had appeared to her in an apparition and
  said the pastor had murdered them. His accusers said that the Devil
  stood beside him on the scaffold as he prayed the Lord's Prayer.
- Bridget Bishop, who was the local tavern keeper and wore lace
  clothes "too elaborate for an honest woman." A neighbor said her
  specter came during his sleep, sat on his stomach, and choked him.
- Giles Corey, an eighty-seven-year-old man, who refused to plead

guilty or not guilty. A procedure known as *peine forte et dure* was used to extract a plea from him. He was stripped, laid on his back, and an iron weight put on him. He was pressed to death without answering his accusers.[5]

- Dorcas Goode, five-year-old daughter of Sarah Goode, who was imprisoned for eight months. The "afflicted" girls accused her of biting and torturing them; they showed a small set of teeth marks on their bodies as evidence against the child.[6]

By the fall of 1692, ministers and citizens were becoming alarmed; the accusations of the girls and the spectral evidence were losing credibility. Increase Mather, the president of Harvard College and the father of Cotton Mather, said, "It is better that ten suspected witches should escape than one innocent person should be condemned."[7] The last trial in January, 1693, found forty-nine of the fifty-three accused innocent. Eventually, all the condemned were reprieved and released.[8]

A No-Nonsense Judge

Another judge, in another town, put his foot down and prevented the hysteria and hate-mongering. That judge was John Howland, ancestor to Seattle storyteller Naomi Baltuck. John Howland came to America on the Mayflower as a servant to Governor Carver. He was a Stranger, or a non-Puritan (who called themselves Saints). John Howland married Elizabeth Tilley, the daughter of a prominent Pilgrim. Naomi's mother, Eleanor, enjoyed saying, "He came as a Stranger and married up!"

Howland became, among other things, a magistrate in Scituate, Massachusetts. The wife of one of Miles Standish's lieutenants was brought before him for witchcraft on complaint of a woman named Dinah Sylvester. He questioned Dinah Sylvester, the accuser:

"What evidence have you of the fact?"

"She appeared to me as a witch."

"In what shape?"

"In the shape of a bear, your honor."

"How far off was the bear?"

"About a stone's throw from the highway."

"What manner of tail did the bear have?"

"I could not tell, your honor, as his head was towards ı

Dinah Sylvester was fined $5 and whipped.[9]

The Lawyer's Advice

(Denmark)

There once was a man who had a cow, which he decided to sell. He went to six different butchers, secured bargains with them, and received ten dollars in advance from each one of them, telling them to come to his house at any time and take the animal away.

In due time, the first butcher came to his house and received the cow. When the rest came and found the barn empty, they became angry and had him summoned to appear in court.

The man went about every day trying to think of some manner in which he could settle this difficult affair, but without being able to find a way out of his troubles. At length he became quite desperate, and in this state of mind appeared in town on the day appointed. When he walked through the streets, looking considerably perplexed, he was hailed by a lawyer who happened to see him from his window, and who observed that he was much oppressed.

"What ails you, my friend?" inquired the lawyer, running into the street and catching the man by his arm.

"It will be of little use for me to tell you," answered he, "because I need a friend who can both turn and twist things around."

"Why," exclaimed the lawyer, "that is my very occupation!" Whereupon he seized the man firmly by the collar and pulled him into the house.

Now the sinner made a confession before him, telling him how it had all happened. Could the lawyer help him out of this difficulty? "Yes," was the answer, "and very easily, too: when you are brought into the courtroom, and the questioning begins, you must answer only 'Oh, pshaw!' Whatever they say to you, you must make no other reply."

When the man was brought before the judge, and the question was put to him whether he had sold the cow to all six butchers as reported, he answered, "Oh, pshaw!"

The judge looked at him over his glasses and repeated, "I ask you whether you sold your cow to these six men and received in advance ten dollars from each of them?"

"Oh, pshaw!" said the man again. Now the judge became excited; however, he stepped forward and shouted into his ear, "Did you sell your cow to these six men?"

The man bent forward and yelled into the judge's ear, "Oh psh-a-aw!"

Since he looked quite sincere, and no other reply could be had from him, the judge turned to the six men, saying, "There is no way in which you can be righted, my friends. This man is insane, and all that we can do is let him go. You may go," concluded he. "Oh, pshaw!" promptly was the reply. The policemen grasped him by the collar and kicked him out of the courtroom.

The lawyer watched the street from his window, and as soon as he saw his friend trudging along, he called him in. The man stopped and gazed at him. "Come in!" called the lawyer. "I must be paid for the good advice I gave you."

"Oh, pshaw!" answered the man, trudging homeward.

SOURCES:

- Bay, J. Christian. *Danish Fairy and Folk Tales*. New York and London: Harper and Brothers Publishers, 1899.
- Briggs, Katharine M. "Pierre Patelin." In *A Dictionary of British Folktales*. Bloomington, Ind.: Indiana University Press, 1970. A man who owes a merchant money is advised by his lawyer to feign insanity by crying "bea" in court.
- Randolph, Vance. "Rick Tyler and the Lawyer." In *Who Blowed Up the Church House? and other Ozark Folk Tales*. New York: Columbia University Press, 1952. A man caught stealing chickens is advised by his lawyer to b-a-a like a sheep in court.
- Sadhu, S. L. "The Clever Lawyer and the Cleverer Client." In *Folktales from Kashmir*. New York and Bombay: Asia Publishing House, 1962. Client who lost cotton in warehouse fire shouts "kapas" or cotton.
- Walker, Barbara K. *The Dancing Palm Tree and Other Nigerian Folktales*. New York: *Parent's*, 1968. Client calls "Rhee."
- Ausubel, Nathan. "The Discerning Judge." In *Treasury of Jewish Folklore*. New York: Crown Publishers, Inc., 1989. A young man who regrets a sale and wants to have it nullified is advised by his attorney to eat some dates and spit the pits in the judge's face. The judge decides the man is not mentally deficient but "just plain impudent."

COMMENTS:

This story contains two widely held opinions: first, that attorneys routinely advise their clients to lie; second, that defendants routinely escape punishment by pleading insanity. As to the first, despite popular opinion, it is unusual for attorneys to cheat to win. Attorneys who encourage deception are violating the law and their professional code of ethics. Any attorney that is certain that his witness gave perjured testimony must report that fact to the judge. The adversary system helps the legal profession police itself. An unethical attorney would be quickly detected by opposing council and reported to the bar association.

Concerning the insanity defense, it is unpopular because the public believes that it is used indiscriminantly and allows guilty criminals to escape punishment. Part of the problem is that it is difficult to understand legally and medically. There are no medical tests that give certain diagnoses; psychiatrists give conflicting opinions; and mental illness seems easy to fake. Consequently, the insanity defense is intertwined with complex moral, legal, and medical issues and has a long, controversial history.

The Insanity Defense
"M'NAGHTEN'S CASE"

The central issue in the criminal justice system is culpability: whether a person is guilty and should be punished for an act. The insanity defense, when successful, allows a person to escape punishment. However, the defendant may be confined in a mental hospital for a long time.

The roots of our insanity defense began in England in 1843. A man named Daniel M'Naghten suffered from delusions that he was being persecuted by the Pope and Prime Minister Peel. He tried to gun down the Prime Minister, but instead shot and killed Peel's secretary. At trial, nine medical experts testified for the defense that M'Naghten was insane. The presiding judge, Lord Chief Justice Tindal, told the jury, "The question to be determined is whether at the time the act in question was committed, the prisoner had or had not the use of his understanding, so as to know that he was doing a wrong or wicked act."[1] The jury returned a verdict of "Not guilty, on the ground of insanity." The verdict caused a furor in England. A popular verse said:

> *Ye people of England: exult and be glad.*
> *For you're now at the will of the merciless mad.*[2]

The fifteen members of the judiciary were summoned to the House of Lords to answer questions about the insanity defense. Lord Chief Justice Tindal said that jurors should be told that every person is presumed sane, and the burden is placed on the accused to prove insanity. He set forth the famous M'Naghten Rule: a person is not responsible for his criminal actions when he does not know the nature and quality of his act or does not know the act was wrong. The defendant's inability to control his conduct is irrelevant. In the United States, the M'Naghten rule has been the basis for the insanity defense. However, the defense is legislated by each state so there is a wide variation.

Some states expanded the M'Naghten Rule to the Brawner Rule: a person is not responsible, if, as a result of mental disease or defect, he lacks substantial capacity to appreciate the wrongfulness of his conduct or to conform his conduct to the requirements of law. In stating that not everyone can 'conform his conduct,' the Brawner Rule opens up issues of self-control and irresistible impulse. These types of legal definition are among the reasons the insanity defense has been hard to understand. A celebrated trial in 1982 brought all of the problems into the spotlight, and threatened to abolish the defense.

The John Hinckley Trial

On March 30, 1981, John W. Hinckley, Jr. fired six shots in an attempt to assassinate President Ronald Reagan. He hit the President, Press Secretary James Brady, a policeman, and a Secret Service Agent, all of whom survived. The attack had been recorded on videotape, which was shown repeatedly on television and introduced at the trial.

The trial was held in the spring of 1982, and Hinckley entered a plea of not guilty due to insanity. Hinckley was charged with thirteen crimes, three of which were federal crimes; therefore the judge ruled the trial would be governed by federal rules. The defense had a big advantage under federal rules, because the prosecution had to prove Hinckley's sanity beyond a reasonable doubt. In addition, the test for insanity was the Brawner Rule.

The trial became a battleground of opposing psychiatrists. Hinckley's wealthy father hired psychiatrists to testify for the defense. They introduced evidence of Hinckley's mental disorder, including his obsession with movie star Jodie Foster. They diagnosed Hinckley as suffering from a major depressive disorder and schizophrenia; therefore not responsible for his acts.

The prosecution's psychiatrist said that Hinckley was spoiled, lazy, and fame-seeking. Although he suffered from personality disorders, he was not so impaired that he could not appreciate the wrongfulness of his conduct or conform his conduct to the requirements of law.[3]

At the end of the trial, the judge read pages of instructions to the jury including the Brawner Rule. They were told if Hinckley was found not guilty by reason of insanity, he would be committed to a mental hospital, and released only if the court finds that he is unlikely to injure himself or others. The jury verdict was "not guilty by reason of insanity."

Reforms and Changes in the Insanity Defense

The outrage over the Hinckley acquittal resulted in attacks on the insanity defense. Hearings were held in the Senate and the House; bills were introduced to limit and reform the defense. In addition, thirty-eight states changed their laws. Some of the changes that occurred were:

- A majority of states narrowed the insanity test to the old M'Naghten Rule of "Can't tell right from wrong." The American Psychiatric

Association recommended that "the irresistible impulse or failure to exercise self-control should not be recognized as a form of mental impairment."

- Eight states added a new "guilty but mentally ill" plea to reduce insanity acquittals. The accused could be found mentally ill but still declared guilty and punished.

- Twelve states shifted the burden of proving insanity to the defendant.

- Twenty-five states made it harder for the people acquitted for insanity to gain release from mental hospitals.[4]

All of these changes occurred in spite of evidence that the public fears about massive acquittals were unfounded. For example, the insanity study published in the *Bulletin of the American Academy of Psychiatry and the Law* reported that in eight states between 1967 and 1987, the insanity defense was used in less than one percent of all criminal cases; only one-fourth of resulted in acquittal. The study said that the vast majority of the people who used the insanity defense were seriously mentally ill.[5]

A Robber I Will Be

(Majorca)

Once, on the island of Majorca and in the city of Arta, there lived a boy named Pablo. When Pablo was seven years old, his father died. His father's will stated that Pablo must be allowed to choose his own profession; his mother vowed to respect his wishes.

Pablo was sent to school, but he did not like it. If he went, he went late. He talked; he teased; he taunted the other boys. Neither the teachers nor his mother could make him behave. His mother tried candy, pleas, tears. His teachers tried threats, detention, whippings. Pablo did as he pleased.

When he was twelve years old, his mother said, "Son, I just give up. You seem determined to do whatever you want to do. Your father said to let you choose the work that pleased you. What do you choose? Do you want to be a priest?"

"Ha!" replied Pablo. "You can't expect me to wear a long face and a robe."

"Then do you want to be a lawyer?"

"Ha! You can't expect me to study for years and work long hours."

"Then do you want to be a doctor?"

"Ha! You can't expect me to hand out castor oil and pills to sick people."

"Well, my strong-minded son, what do you want to be?"

Pablo said, "I want to be a robber!"

"What did you say, my dear son?"

"I said, 'I want to be a robber'."

"What did you say, you little brat?"

Pablo said it again, in even a louder voice. "I want to be a robber. I won't have to go to school. I can work when I want. I will make a lot of money. And my father said I can choose what I will be!"

His mother picked up her hairbrush and chased him around the room. But Pablo ran faster and kept shouting, "I want to be a robber and a robber I will be." When she could not catch him or quiet him, she left the room in tears.

Time went by, but little changed for Pablo; he still skipped school and refused to study. If his mother tried to correct his unruly behavior, Pablo began to shout, "I want to be a robber and a robber I will be." These words always caused his mother to stop her discipline and run from the room in tears.

Years went by: Pablo turned sixteen. He announced, "I have had enough of this life. I am a man and ready to make my way in life. I am off to the mountain, the Beak of Ferrutz, where there is a band of robbers living in a cave. Tomorrow, I will join up with them and become the biggest, baddest robber in all of Majorca."

His mother ran from the room crying, and went to seek the advice of her deceased husband's brother. Her brother-in-law said, "As luck would have it, the captain of the robbers is a boyhood friend. He would do anything for me, and I'm sure he will not be happy babysitting a boy like Pablo. I have a plan to make Pablo regret his life as a robber. Let me write a letter to the Robber Captain."

The next morning, Pablo started out for the Beak of Ferrutz with a little satchel his mother packed with clean underwear, socks, and hankies. He carried his uncle's letter of introduction. He did not know what was in the letter because he had not learned to read.

He reached the foot of the mountain called the Beak of Ferrutz. "It does look like the beak of a big bird," thought Pablo. "All those big rocks will be good hiding places where I can rob travelers. What a life I am going to lead!"

But suddenly, from behind one of those big rocks, three men jumped out and grabbed young Pablo. They searched his pockets and emptied out his satchel. "Where's your money?" they demanded.

"I don't have any money," the boy replied. "But I will soon. I've come to join your band. I want to be a robber too."

The trio just laughed and laughed until Pablo showed them his letter. "You better be nice to me or you will be sorry. Now take me to the Captain."

The men dragged the boy up a narrow path between huge boulders. Pablo complained and bragged the entire journey. The opening to the cave was hidden behind thickets. The men pushed Pablo inside the cave and down in front of a man seated on a cask of wine. "Well, what have you brought me? A rich mama's boy who will fetch a big ransom?" asked the Captain.

"Not this one. He wants to join us," explained one of the robbers. "He even has a letter of introduction."

The Captain read the letter and asked Pablo, "So you want to be a robber? I knew your father; a fine man from a fine family. What would he say about this robber business?"

Pablo spoke boldly, "He said in his will that I could choose my own profession. And a robber I will be!"

"I will do as your uncle asked and I will take you into the band. Señor Pablo, a robber you will be, but you will do it my way. You may not have obeyed your mother or your teachers, but you will obey me. Agreed?"

"Agreed."

Pablo's stomach was empty at mealtime, and he rushed to share the pot of beans. "No food for you," the Captain told him. "You haven't brought anything for the pot." Later, as Pablo fell asleep on the cave floor, he heard one of the robbers talking. "If I had enough money, I would buy a farm. All day, I would tend sheep and in the evening, I would eat a meal with my wife and children and sleep in a bed. I would be happy all my days."

The next morning, the Captain stood at the mouth of the cave, scanning the Plain of Petra and the Black Mountains. He saw a man coming up from one of the small towns, carrying a lamb around his neck. "Pablo," he said. "If you are ready to be a robber, go take the lamb away from that man."

Pablo answered, "Yes, sir." And then he added, "I need a sword." They brought him an old sword and sheath, and he shined them until they gleamed. Away he went down the path.

When he was out of sight, the Captain chuckled, "That old sword won't help. He is going to rob big, strong Massot. And Massot will send our little robber running home to his mother."

Pablo ran down the mountainside and found the path where Massot would pass. He placed the sheath in the center of the path, ran down further, and dropped the sword. He hid in the bushes and waited.

Soon, Massot came along carrying his lamb. He spied the sheath, picked it up, and examined it. Having no sword and so no need for a sheath, Massot tossed it in the bushes and continued walking. But further on the path, he found the shiny sword. "This must be the sword that fit in the sheath I threw away. I'll fetch it." Massot put the lamb on the ground so he could run quicker.

Pablo popped out of the bushes, scooped up the lamb, and was back to the cave before Massot discovered his loss. The robbers were impressed. "Didn't he beat you?" they asked, because they knew about Massot's temper and strength.

The big man searched for the lost lamb. When he could not find it, he returned to the shepherd where he had bought the lamb. "Did that lamb come back?"

"What lamb?"

"The one I just bought and carried off," said Massot and he explained about the sword, sheath, and missing lamb. They searched the flock, with no results because, of course, the lamb was already simmering in the robbers' stewpot. Massot said, "I can't wait to find it. I must have a lamb for a wedding feast tomorrow."

"Take another," said the shepherd. "The missing one will return; if not, you can pay me later." Massot gave him thanks and threw another lamb across his shoulders and went down the road where he had gone before.

The Captain saw Massot with a new lamb. "Quick, Pablo. Here is another chance to prove you are a robber." Pablo bounded out of the cave and hid in the bushes along the roadside. As soon as he saw Massot, Pablo made the small cries of a lost lamb. "Baaa! Baaa! Baaa!"

Massot shouted, "There you are, little one. Baa! Come to me. Baaa!" He put down the lamb he was carrying, and began rushing through the bushes. Pablo ran to another bush and called, "Baa!"

Massot ran and called, "Don't run away, little one. Baa!" Pablo ran and Massot followed, farther and farther away from the lamb. When Massot collapsed in fatigue, the boy robber circled back. He picked up the animal and was in the cave before Massot had even caught his breath. "Done!" he announced in triumph to the astonished Captain.

Meanwhile, poor Massot returned to the shepherd; he was tired, frustrated, but mostly confused. When the shepherd saw the big man's empty arms, he exclaimed, "You mean you lost another one?"

"Yes. I'm just sick about it. But I must have a lamb to roast for the wedding." The shepherd hoisted a third sheep on Massot's shoulders. Away he went. The sun was soon to set.

The Captain spied Massot. "Pablo, your day's work is not done."

He pointed at the lamb. "Run and get it and don't come back without it."
Pablo scampered out of the cave and hid in the bushes before Massot got
there. He pulled off his shoes. When, Massot came along, Pablo hit the
leather soles of his shoes together. Whap-whap-whap! Stopping to listen
to the sound, Massot declared, "That's my two lambs butting their heads
together and playing. I'll sneak up on them."

Once again, he put his lamb on the ground to chase Pablo
through the bushes. Whap-whap-whap! The boy lured the man though
the bushes until the sun set. Massot stumbled and fell. Pablo ran quickly
through the darkness and captured the lamb. He arrived at the cave with
the third lamb over his shoulders and his shoes in his hand.

The band of robbers were secretly surprised that Pablo had
stolen three sheep and returned without a beating. They pretended not to
notice. Pablo put the lamb down and ran to join the meal. The lamb stew
was steamy and fragrant. When Pablo dipped the ladle into the pot, he
heard the Captain say, "That's not for you. There's a cold plate of beans
for you."

Pablo sassed back, "I won't eat yesterday's beans when my lamb
stew is dripping off your chin."

The Captain just laughed. "Pablo, you said you would obey me. If
I say 'Eat beans', you will eat beans."

"That's not fair. I ran up and down the mountain all day while
you sat and smoked your pipe."

The Captain just laughed louder. "Fair? You want fair? You want
justice? Well, my son, you have come to the wrong place. Here you get
Thieves' Justice. You steal from Massot; we steal from you."

Pablo responded, "If that's the way it's going to be, a robber's life
is not for me." He was out of the cave, down the mountain, and knocking
on his mother's door before the Captain could bid him farewell. His
mother opened the door. Pablo told her, "A robber I don't want to be. I
have a better plan."

Pablo worked hard to pay for the stolen sheep. Then he worked harder to buy a farm. Then, all day, he tended sheep, and in the evening ate a meal with his wife and children, and slept in a bed. He was happy all his days.

SOURCES:

- Dane, George Ezra, and Beatrice J. Dane. "The Boy Who Would A Robber Be." In *Once There Was and Was Not; Tales and Rhymes from Majorca*. New York: Junior Books, Doubleday, Doran and Co., Inc., 1931.
- Mehdevi, Alexander. "Augustine the Thief." In *Bungling Pedro and Other Majorcan Tales*. New York: Alfred A. Knopf, 1970.
- Campbell, Marie. "The Boy That was Trained to Be a Thief." In *Cloud Walking Country*. Bloomington, Ind.: Indiana University Press, 1958.

COMMENTS:

This story reminds me of an anecdote I heard in college. My roommate, Liz, had a red-haired, witty mother, Mary McKnight Spence. Mary was a second-grade school teacher who loved her students. The student that worried her and amused her the most was a toughy named Patty. One day when Mary asked the class what they wanted to be when they grew up, Patty raised her hand and proudly proclaimed, "A stealer!" Hopefully Patty, like Pablo, was dissuaded from her life of crime.

Juvenile Justice

Throughout the ages, teachers, parents, and community members have puzzled how to handle troublesome children such as Pablo. In 1899, the first juvenile court was established in Illinois. The juvenile justice system was akin to a social agency; the *parens patriae* or "parent of the country," with power to watch over youth who were incapable of protecting themselves. The purpose was to help, rather than punish, children in trouble. In most states, a juvenile proceeding was not a criminal trial, but an informal hearing. Children were treated differently than adults who broke the law.[1]

The landmark case of *In re Gault*, 387 US 1 (1967) examined the issue of whether a juvenile system which held informal hearings was constitutional. In 1964, Gerald Gault was fifteen and living in rural Arizona. He and a friend made an obscene telephone call to a neighbor. The neighbor recognized Gault's voice and called the sheriff; Gault, who was on probation for petty theft, was taken to a juvenile home.

Several informal hearings were held without official notice; the neighbor did not testify. A questionable admission from Gault was the primary basis for the judge's ruling that Gault was a juvenile delinquent. He was ordered to be confined in a reform school until the age of twenty-one. An adult might have been fined up to fifty dollars and sentenced up to two months in jail.[2]

Arizona did not allow an appeal from juvenile proceedings. His parents filed a writ of habeas corpus, a petition challenging the legality of his confinement. When a higher court in Arizona ruled Gault's confinement was legal, the Gault family appealed to the United States Supreme Court on the grounds that the boy had been denied constitutional rights during the juvenile hearing.

The Supreme Court said that juvenile hearings were similar to adult criminal trials because the hearings might result in confinement. Therefore, an absence of constitutional guarantees deprived juveniles of a fair hearing. The Court ruled that the due process clause of the Fourteenth Amendment applies to juvenile proceedings; juveniles are due these rights:

- Notice of the charges. There must be written notice of the facts in time to prepare for the hearing.

- Right to counsel. The child may hire an attorney or have one appointed.

- Right to remain silent. The child does not have to testify, and an involuntary confession cannot not be used as evidence.

- Right to confront witnesses. There must be sworn testimony to support a ruling and an opportunity to cross-examine the witnesses.

Gerald Gault was released from the reformatory, but his appeal had taken three years.[3]

Anansi Drinks Boiling Water

◈

(Jamaica)

As is well known, Anansi, the Spider Man, was lazy and did not tend his garden. His storehouse was usually empty. So when the king called the animals to come and harvest his yams, Anansi thought of a plan to fill his own storehouse.

That night, he went to the king's fields, dug a hole, and covered it with grass. The next morning, Anansi went to the fields with Rat, Bullfrog, Crow, and all the other animals. The animals dug yams, put them in baskets, and carried them to the King's storehouse. But Anansi dug a yam and put it in his basket, then dug a yam and dropped it into the concealed hole. He sang softly:

One for him.
One for me.

The animals were busy digging and carrying; they did not see the tricky Spider Man drop yams in a hole in the ground. They did not hear him sing softly:

One for him.
One for me.

With hard work, the animals cleared the yams from the fields and went home. Anansi waited for darkness and took his family to the hole in the king's field. They made many trips to carry the yams home. Before dawn, the hole was empty and their storehouse was full.

The next morning, Rat saw Anansi's full storehouse. He called to Bullfrog, "Look at all the yams." They called to Crow, "Look at all the yams. They were not there yesterday." Seeing the new path, they followed it from Anansi's storehouse to the king's fields. There they found the big, empty hole. "This is where Anansi was working yesterday. Let's tell the king."

When the king heard and saw the evidence, he called the animals together and summoned Anansi. "Your habits are well known. You do not tend your garden, and yesterday your storehouse was empty. Today your storehouse is full of yams, and there is a path from your storehouse to my yam fields. There is a big hole next to where you worked. Anansi, you are a thief."

"Not me!" said Anansi. "I am innocent."

The king responded, "If you are innocent, you can prove it with a test. All the animals are gathered. We will watch you drink boiling water. If, as you claim, you are innocent, you will not be harmed. But if you are guilty, the boiling water will scald you and you will suffer."

Anansi answered, "Test me. I am innocent."

A king's servant took a steaming pot from the fire, poured boiling water into a calabash, and handed it to Anansi. The animals watched as he took the calabash and lifted it to his lips. He only pretended to taste it. "This water is not hot enough to prove my innocence," he told the crowd. He looked at the sun, high in the sky. "I will put this water into the sun so it can heat up more."

The animals, who had been seated in the hot sun, agreed that Anansi had a good idea. Anansi set the calabash in the center of the circle of animals and joined them to wait. They began to sweat as the sun beat down. Anansi got up and checked the water. "Not hot enough yet," he told the crowd. They waited and sweated as Anansi checked and rechecked. At last, he declared that the water was indeed boiling hot. He lifted the calabash to his lips and drained the contents. The animals gasped in admiration as Anansi wiped his mouth and cried, "Innocent!" Then Anansi went home to his storehouse of fine new yams.

SOURCES:

My version of this story is a blend of the characters and plots of the following sources. Anansi's song is my own addition.

- Sherlock, Philip M. "Anansi and the Crabs." In *Anansi the Spider Man: Jamaican Folk Tales*. New York: Thomas Y. Crowell Co., 1954.
- Courlander, Harold. "Ijapa and the Hot-Water Test." In *Olode the Hunter and Other Tales from Nigeria*. New York: Harcourt, Brace and World, Inc., 1968.

COMMENTS:

Anansi the Spider Man is the beloved rascal of West African folktales. Anansi is sometimes a man, but when things go wrong, he becomes a spider and scurries to his web. He is responsible for many mythological events. In one story, he performs a series of tasks and obtains all the stories from the sky god. In another story, while climbing a tree with a pot containing all the world's wisdom, Anansi drops the pot, which breaks and scatters wisdom to the corners of the world.

When men and women were taken as slaves to the islands of the Caribbean, they brought their stories with them. The characters remained very much alike, but had different names on different islands. In Jamaica, Anansi kept the name he was called by the Ashanti people. He has another name on St. Lucia: he is Compé Czien or Brother Spider.[1]

Like Anansi the spider in Ashanti tales, Ijapa the tortoise is the shrewd, greedy trickster of the Yoruba people of Western Nigeria.

Courlander comments that Ijapa's occasionally triumphant schemes are an African recognition that good and evil exist as part of life. The stories acknowledge that there are elements of whim, accident and amoral forces in nature.[2]

Harold Courlander comments that the occasionally triumphant schemes of Ijapa the Tortoise is an African recognition that good and evil exist as part of life. The stories acknowledge that much of nature is amoral, subject to whim and accident.

Folktales, historical stories, and modern newspaper reports remind us that there have always been tricksters, swindlers, and thieves. Why else would we need laws, courts, and jails? But, sadly, tricksters are not always caught, judges are not always wise, and bad deeds are not always punished. We can cry about the reality of injustice; we can work for the ideal of justice; and sometimes, just to lighten our spirits, we can laugh at a clever trickster and see a little bit of our human nature in him.

Trial by Ordeal

In this story, Anansi undergoes trial by boiling water. In another African folktale, "Why Leopard Has Spots," by Peggy Appiah in *Tales of an Ashanti Father*, the animals had to submit to trial by fire. The animals leaped over a fire to show they had not eaten stolen garden eggs. Having a full stomach, Leopard, the thief, fell into the flames, and the fire burned spots in his fur.

Trial by fire is also found among the Afro-American tales of Uncle Remus. In "The Fire Test" by Julius Lester in *More Tales from Uncle Remus*, the animals had to jump over a fire because they believed the one who ate Brer Rabbit's children would fall into it. Brer Fox, who was trembling, took a long running start. By the time he reached the fire, he was tired and jumped "smack in the fire." And not a tear was shed.

These folktales reflect the historical use of trial by ordeal, one of the most ancient methods of seeking truth. The ordeal was based on a belief that God could be called upon to divine the truth of the matter in question. The accused was forced to perform an almost impossible and dangerous act. Only by surviving unharmed was innocence proven.

There have been many forms of ordeal throughout the ages. A trial called the "bitter waters of testing" is described in Numbers 5:11-29. If an Israelite husband thought that his wife was unfaithful, he brought her before the priest, along with a "jealousy offering of barley." The priest poured holy water into an earthen vessel, and added some dust from the base of the altar. Then he shaved the woman's head. While the woman held the jealousy offering, the priest held the water of testing. He spoke an "oath of cursing" to her: if she had defiled herself, the water "shall enter into her and cause bitter pain, and her body shall swell, and her thigh shall fall away." Then the priest wrote the curses and dipped them in the water. Then the woman drank the water to prove if she was defiled or pure.[3]

In ancient Greece, people of high rank were subjected to the ordeal of walking barefoot through fire or over hot iron. In the play *Antigone*, the Guard offers to walk over fire to prove his innocence.[4]

In England, during the eleventh and twelfth centuries, both boiling and cold water were used for ordeal. Boiling water was used to heat a stone the accused was forced to take out of the water. Other suspects, particularly those accused of witchcraft, were tied up and flung into a cold pond. They were innocent if they floated, guilty if they sank. Ordeals were frequently supervised by priests and administered during church mass.

The English trial by ordeal was abolished shortly after the signing of the Magna Carta. The Magna Carta was a document of liberties issued in 1212 by King John. Barons and churchmen coerced the King to sign in order to protect their rights. The Magna Carta has served as a historical touchstone of liberty for England and subsequently, the United States. In

1215, at the Fourth Lateran Council, the Church also forbade priests to take part in ordeals.[5]

Sharing Crops

❧

(United States)

After John got his freedom, he went to the owner of the big cotton plantation. "I am a good farmer, why, I could plant rocks and they would sprout big and tall. Will you rent me a piece of land?" asked John.

The owner said, "Sure, John, if you'll share the crop with me." He showed John a little piece of land down by the river.

John set right to work plowing the land. But as John plowed, he thought and he worried, "That man starved me when I was a slave; he'll starve me now that I'm a cropper."

When the owner came down to the field to check the plowing, John asked him, "What part of the crop is yours and what part is mine?" John expected the man to say, "You take half and I'll take half," or some such thing. But the man didn't even look John in the eye. He just said, "The top half of the crop is mine and the bottom half is yours."

"That will suit me just fine," replied John.

John knew the owner had cotton on the brain, and John knew the man planned to take all the cotton from the top and leave the roots for him. But John didn't plant cotton; he planted potatoes.

A couple of months later, the owner strolled toward the field expecting to see it white with cotton. John headed him off by the road. "You keep the tops and I keep the bottoms? Right?" reminded the cropper. "That's right, John," said the owner, about three seconds before he saw the field of potato plants.

The man threw a fit. Finally, he stomped off and yelled over his shoulder, "Keep them tops. But next year, it will be different."

Next year at plowing time, John went to see the owner. "Will you rent me that piece of land? This year it will be different."

The owner answered, "You can bet it will be different. I'd like to rotate the agreement." The owner didn't look John in the eye. "This year, I'll take the bottoms and you take the tops."

"That will suit me just fine," said John.

John went down by the river and plowed the field. While he was plowing, he thought and he worried. "That owner is the kind of man who would flip a coin in the air and call out, 'Heads I win, and tails you lose.'"

Several months later, the owner strolled towards the field, expecting to see a crop of potatoes. John headed him off at the road. "Bottoms for you and tops for me? That right?" asked John.

"That's right!" said the owner just about three steps before he saw the field. The whole field was planted in corn.

"When do you want me to deliver the roots of them corn stalks?" shouted John to the owner as he marched away.

The next year when John went up to the plantation, the owner looked John straight in the eye. "Not more tops or bottoms," he said. "I'll take the same as you, half and half."

SOURCES:

- Courlander, Harold. "Sharing the Crops." In *Terrapin's Pot of Sense*. New York: Henry Holt and Co., 1957. The plantation owner and sharecropper share potatoes, oats, and corn.
- Eddins, A. W. "Sheer Crops." In *Texas Folk and Folklore XXVI*. Ed. Mody C. Boatright. Dallas: Southern Methodist University Press, 1954. Br'er Bear and Br'er Rabbit share potatoes, oats, and corn.
- Grimm, Jakob Ludwig Karl and Wilheim Karl Grimm. "The Peasant

and the Devil." In *Grimms' Tales for Young and Old*. New York: Doubleday, 1977. A peasant and the Devil divide turnips and wheat.

- Sanfield, Steve. "Tops and Bottoms." In *The Adventures of High John the Conqueror*. New York: Orchard Books, Division of Franklin Watts, 1989. Reprint, Little Rock, Ark.: August House Publishers, Inc., 1996. High John and Boss share potatoes, wheat, and corn.

- This type of tale is so prevalent that in *The Storyteller's Sourcebook*, Margaret Read McDonald listed twenty-six variants under the motif K171.1 Deceptive Crop Division.

Further information about "John" and "High John the Conqueror"

- Hurston, Zora Neale. "High John the Conqueror." In *Mother Wit from the Laughing Barrel*. Englewood Cliffs, N. J.: Prentice Hall, 1973.
- Oster, Harry. "Negro Humor: John and Old Master." In *Mother Wit from the Laughing Barrel*. Englewood, N. J.: Prentice Hall, 1973.
- Levine, Lawrence W. "The Slave As Trickster." In *Black Culture and Black Consciousness*. New York: Oxford University Press, 1977.

COMMENTS:

John was the trickster hero of slaves in the South. He sometimes improved his lot by clever deception, maybe getting a little more food. He sometimes outwitted the Master. Sometimes, he even won his freedom with trickery. One thing was certain, John could always make people laugh with his antics. Amid the suffering of slavery, laughter was a precious thing. A saying comes down from those years of bondage: "If I laugh loud enough, maybe no one will hear me cry."

In this tale, John is a freed slave. He obviously did not leave for the northern cities as did thousands of freed slaves. Emancipation had resulted in some changes, but John was stuck with his old master, who still had the land. And the old master was stuck with John, who still had the muscle and skill. Therefore the two had to learn to arrange sharecropping.

This tale has several possible endings. Usually, after the would-be cheater discovered he had been cheated again, the arrangement and relationship ended. For example, Sanfield's High John did not ask to rent again because Boss probably would not deal with him. I like the more optimistic ending of Corlander's African tale where the plantation owner agreed to a fair division. Perhaps the owner realized, however begrudgingly, that he needed John and John was not just a dumb farm animal he could cheat.

The Slave Mutiny Aboard the Amistad

For a legal comment to accompany "Sharing Crops," I chose the mutiny on the Amistad because the court rulings gave a small measure of justice amid the injustice of slavery. In 1839, slavery was still legal in the United States; the Emancipation Proclamation was not signed by Lincoln until 1863. However, it was illegal to bring additional slaves into the United States from other countries.

In the late summer of 1839, a long, black schooner, the *Amistad*, was spotted drifting off the coast of Long Island, New York. On board were two Spanish sailors and slaves from Africa. When the ship was seized by a U.S. frigate and taken ashore, the Spanish sailors reported a mutiny by the slaves and murder of the captain, cook, and two crew members. The Africans were jailed. The Spanish government asked for a return of the *Amistad* and the cargo of slaves.

The Africans were imprisoned for many months before trial on murder and piracy. No one could speak or understand their language, so their story remained untold. Then a Yale professor met with the Africans and learned to count in their language. Next, he went to the docks in New York and searched for any slave who could understand the counting. He found an African who had been kidnapped from Africa and could speak the prisoners' tongue. At last, the prisoners were able to report what had happened to them.

One of the men was called Singbe (or Cinque in Spanish). He said that earlier in the year, he had been kidnapped from his rice fields in Africa, near Sierra Leone. He had been held in a slave stockade with people kidnapped from other tribes. Singbe had been shipped in chains to Havana, Cuba, with several hundred slaves.

He was sold at auction and loaded aboard the *Amistad* with forty-eight other slaves. The *Amistad* set sail for a three-hundred-mile trip down the coast to Puerto Principe. After the cook told the slaves that they were going to be eaten, Singbe used a nail to unlock his chains and free the other slaves. They overcame the crew and killed the captain and the cook. Taking charge, Singbe ordered the remaining two crew members to sail the ship back to Africa. During the day, the Spanish sailors navigated toward the east, but at night, they reversed their course and headed toward Cuba. The *Amistad* floundered in wind and currents for two months before it was discovered.

The abolitionists were fighting to end slavery and the newspapers followed the case closely. When the Africans' story was heard, many people cried out that the homicides were justifiable. A group of abolitionists hired lawyers to defend the Africans. The defense team included the ex-president of the United States John Quincy Adams.

At trial, the defense argued that the Africans were free men, captured in violation of Spanish law, because slave trading had been prohibited since 1820. They had rightfully taken action to free themselves from the horrors of slavery. The court agreed and found the defendants innocent.

The prosecution appealed the case to the U.S. Supreme Court, where five of the nine judges were Southerners who had formerly owned slaves. Adams presented the oral argument for the defense. The Supreme Court upheld the lower court's decision. The schooner was returned to its

Spanish owners, and the Africans were freed to return to their homes in Africa.

No help came from the government to supply passage for the Africans. Abolitionists and black church members helped set up a dormitory in a barn in Farmington, Connecticut. The "Amistads" farmed and made tablecloths and napkins to raise money. At last, they sailed back to Africa, accompanied by an interracial group of missionaries.[1]

The Money Tree

❦

(Apache)

One day Coyote was out walking. He saw a shady tree so he sat down under it. Coyote was always in trouble and always playing tricks. He had two or three dollars with him. He took his money and placed it on different branches. Coyote swept the ground clean and sat in the shade. Then he waited.

Along came some prospectors with several pack mules, blankets, and plenty of provisions. They came upon Coyote sitting under the tree right by the path. The prospectors asked him. "What are you doing here?"

"I am watching my tree all day long," he told them.

They asked, "What's on that tree? Is it money?"

"Yes, the tree is very valuable. This is the only tree that grows money. There is no other tree like it anywhere."

They questioned him, "What do you have to do to get money?"

"I wait while the money ripens on the tree. It ripens every day at noon. Then I shake the tree and get all the money I want. It falls from the branches." Coyote stood up and shook the tree. Two or three dollars fell to the ground and he put them in his pocket.

"Sure enough, it bears money," the prospectors said. "We want that tree. We will buy it from you."

He told them, "You can't give me enough for it."

"We'll give you everything we've got. You can have the pack

mules, the blankets, everything. We will just get off our mules and hand them over. You take it all," they said.

Coyote hesitated a little as if he didn't want to do it. Then he said, "If I'm going to trade with you, there's just one thing you must do. The money is not ripe yet—you must wait until tomorrow at noon. Then you can shake the tree and have all the money you want. But if you shake the tree before then, you will spoil the whole thing—you won't get much money."

So the men got off and shook hands with Coyote. Then Coyote got on a mule and began to drive the others alongside him down the path. The prospectors watched him until he went over the big blue mountains. Then they sat under the tree and watched and talked about all the money they would get. That night they camped under the tree, and the next day they waited until noon. They shook the tree. No money fell down. They pounded the tree. No money fell down.

Some decided to find Coyote. They went in the direction he had gone over the mountains. But some men stayed under the tree to wait for the money to ripen. I hear they are sitting there still.

SOURCES:

• Opler, Morris Edward, ed. "Coyote Sells the Money Tree." In *Myths and Tales of the Chiricahua Apache Indians*. Millwood, New York: Kraus Reprint Co., 1976; "Coyote Sells the Money Tree." In *Myths and Legends of the Lipan Apache Indians*. New York: Augustin Publisher, 1940.

• Goodwin, Grenville. "Coyote Steals Wheat." In *Myths and Tales of the White Mountain Apache*. New York: American Folk-lore Society, J. J. Augustin Publisher, 1932. Coyote plays a series of tricks including selling a money tree to soldiers.

• Druts, Yefim, and Alexei Gessler. "Would You Like to Be Rich?" In

Russian Gypsy Tales. New York: Interlink Books, 1992. A gypsy tricks a peasant into planting gold coins, keeps the coins, and explains that there is no crop because of no rain.

- Kaula, Edna Mason. "Kalulu and His Money Farm." In *African Village Folktales*. Cleveland and New York: The World Publishing Company, 1968. Kalulu the Hare gets into mischief when he takes the king's bag of cowrie shells (money) and promises to grow more.
- Pino-Saaverda, Yolanda. "Pedro Urdemales Cheats Two Horsemen." In *Folktales of Chile*. Chicago: University of Chicago Press, 1968. Pedro plays a number of tricks including hanging coins on a hawthorn bush.
- Jagendorf, M. A., and Virginia Weng. "A True Money Tree." In *The Magic Boat and Other Chinese Folk Stories*. New York: Vanguard Press, 1980. A poor man named Long Life prospers as a farmer because he says his father left him a "money tree with two trunks and ten branches." The money tree is his two arms and ten fingers which work hard farming.

COMMENTS:

Tricksters are beloved in folktales. The trickster tale is especially prominent among native peoples in North America. Coyote tales are the most common. Everyone laughs at Coyote's tricks and foolishness. The dire consequences of his bad behavior show the outcome of bragging, stealing, and laziness. These tales often provide children with an example of how not to behave. "See what happens?" the elders say, "Don't be like Coyote."

Like many legendary tricksters, Coyote has a dual character. Sometimes, as in a tale about stealing fire for humankind, he is wise and wily. Sometimes, as in "Coyote and the Horned Toad," he is a stupid clown who is outwitted by the other animals. Clarkson and Cross, in their informative text, *World Folktales*, report that the Navajo have two names for Coyote's dual character; "Coyote" and "Trotting Coyote."[1] He also has two trails of life which he can travel; one is white and the other is yellow. These paths run side by side in a spiral. When Coyote travels the white trail, he is good and wise. On the yellow trail, he is deceitful and evil.[2]

In this tale, there is seeming injustice because Coyote is successful in his swindle. A thieving trickster like Coyote might occasionally escape punishment, but he always is punished by the reputation he has earned. His neighbors distrust him; doors are locked against him; he is always on the run. He remains outside the community, like a coyote snatching offal in the desert.

On the other hand, this successful swindle is not unjust if seen from Coyote's perspective. Historically, miners, soldiers, and settlers were swarming through his homelands, digging in sacred mountains, building forts, and killing game. There must have been some justice for Coyote to outwit this gullible and greedy group who were willing to believe money grew on trees. Perhaps in this cautionary tale the message is, "Don't be stupid like the prospectors who think money comes without work."

Mine Swindles

In this folktale, Coyote swindled the prospectors; in the history of the Old West, prospectors often swindled each other. A frequent type of fraud was "salting a mine" with gold and silver in order to con the buyer into thinking it was valuable. For example, gold dust was shot into the mine with a shotgun.

One famous salting was in the Comstock field in Nevada during the 1860s. Silver nuggets were found in the North Ophir claim, and the mine stock went sky high until one of the nuggets was found with an inscription "...ted States of..." printed on it. The mine promoters had cut up silver dollars, beat the pieces into nuggets, and salted the claim.[3]

The Money-Making Machine

In this folktale, Coyote grew money on trees; in history, swindlers printed money with machines. In the 1800s money-making machines were quite popular. The swindler would demonstrate the process by placing a plain piece of paper inside one compartment of the machine and a genuine bill in another compartment. The machine took six hours to duplicate the genuine bill with a new serial number. The con and victim waited by the machine until a new bill was printed, and the victim was sent to the bank to see if the bill was accepted. Meanwhile, the con man set up the machine again by loading a fresh bill into a secret drawer. When he closed the drawer, he pressed a pin which dropped the secret drawer to be discovered six hours later.

After the victim returned from the bank reassured that the printed bill was passable, the victim convinced the con man to sell the machine. The con man reluctantly sold, but only because the machine was so slow.

After the con man left, the victim waited six hours and found the previously concealed, genuine bill. The machine was reset. Six more hours passed before the drawer revealed a blank piece of paper, reality dawned, and the con man had a head start out of town.

"Count" Victor Lustig was the leading practitioner of the money-making machine swindle. The Count sold the machine to bankers, businessmen, gangsters, and small-town lawmen. He was born in Czechoslovakia in 1890 and came to the United States as a well-established rogue; for example, he twice sold the Eiffel Tower. The Count suckered such famous gangsters as Legs Diamond and Al Capone with bonus stocks and fraudulent schemes.[4]

Awaiting trial for counterfeiting, the Count escaped out of the lavatory window on an upper floor of the jail. When the crowd on the street spotted him, he pretended to wash the windows as he worked his way down each floor. But his grand scams came to a halt when he was later recaptured, brought to trial, and died in prison.

The Thief Who Slid Down a Moonbeam
&

(Turkey)

One night, the Hodja was sleeping soundly in his bed. A noise on the roof woke him. "Wife," he whispered as he nudged her awake. "Wife! I hear someone walking on our roof." His sleepy wife sat up and listened. "It must be a thief."

The Hodja looked around his modest house and replied, "If he finds anything worth stealing, let's steal it back!"

His wife whispered, "I am afraid. Please, catch him."

The Hodja replied, "I have a plan; just play along with me." She nodded, and the Hodja said in a loud voice, "Dear wife, I have been looking around at all our wealth. I never told you how I came to be so rich, did I?"

"No, my dear husband, you have never told me. How did you come to be so rich?"

"I used to be a thief. I would go into people's houses at night. And the reason I was so successful was that I used magic. I would say a magic word seven times and then slide down a moonbeam right into the house. It worked every time."

The wife asked, "What is your magic word?"

"Hodji Bodji!"

Up on the roof, there was a muttering of words and a shuffling of feet. Suddenly, a thief landed in the courtyard outside. He lay stunned on the ground, clutching for a moonbeam, and repeating over and over, "Hodji Bodji, Hodji Bodji."

The Hodja ran outside, grabbed the thief by the scruff of his neck, and led him away for punishment.

It is easier to earn a living than to slide down a moonbeam and say "Hodji Bodji" seven times.

SOURCES:

This story is a blended retelling from these sources:

- Berson, Harold. *The Thief Who Hugged A Moonbeam.* New York: Seabury Press, 1972.
- Downing, Charles. *Tales of the Hodja.* New York: Henry Z. Walck, Inc., 1965.
- Jablow, Alta, and Carl Withers. "The Man Who Climbed Down a Moonbeam." In *The Man in the Moon: Sky Tales from Many Lands* New York: Holt, Rinehart, and Winston, 1969.

COMMENTS:

No collection of folktales would be complete without tales of Nasredden Hodja. His name has various spellings; a hodja was a Moslem priest, teacher, and scholar. Similar to Coyote and Anansi, the Hodja appears to be both naive and wise. He is usually depicted as short, round man, riding a donkey, and wearing a gigantic turban. There are hundreds of short, pithy Hodja stories; most of the plots are found repeated in every country.

In my retelling, I have added the words "hodji bodji" after consulting with storyteller Tom Galt. Tom went to high school in Pakistan and is familiar with Eastern culture. "Hodji bodji" is a man who has made a pilgrimage to Mecca. I chose the words because they are impossible to repeat seven times as the story demands.

Tom is a member of the Bardic Order in the Society for Creative

Anachronism. When he dons his pointed ears and pointed shoes to tell a story, he looks like a leprechaun. When he winds on his turban, he looks like the Hodja himself.

Stupid Crook Tricks

The thief in this story appears incredibly stupid to believe he can slide down a moonbeam. But in reality, criminals often do stupid things. When I was a deputy prosecutor, I often heard hapless defense attorneys arguing to juries, "My client wouldn't be dumb enough to…" But I have heard of criminals who:

- tried to return stolen merchandise for cash.
- drove around in a stolen red car with a personal license plate "Foxy."
- tried to escape police by running through a dark park with shoes that had flashing lights in the heels.
- got stuck headfirst in a chimney while trying to enter a house.
- got locked inside a restaurant during a burglary and had to call 911.

Is it lack of intelligence, lack of judgment from drugs or alcohol, or a mixture of greed and daring?

One of my favorite bumbling criminals from history is Al Jennings. In the 1890s, in the wild Oklahoma Territory, Jennings decided that he and his three brothers would become train robbers. His first attempt was dangerous and comic; he stood on the tracks and flagged the engineer to stop. He was ignored and nearly crushed. His second attempt was equally unsuccessful. Al and his brothers rode horseback alongside a train, firing their guns as a signal to halt. The engineer gave a friendly salute and kept steaming onward.

After two of the brothers were shot in a saloon fight, Al and his brother Frank joined up with three other outlaws. Al led the gang to their only successful train robbery. They happened upon a train at a water stop and got sixty dollars. Al and Frank were captured singlehandedly by lawman Bud Ledbetter. Ledbetter told the Jennings boys to drop their guns and tie themselves up. They were given life sentences; Al got out in five years and Frank seven. After his release, Al went on the lecture circuit with his own accounts of being the "last of the Western outlaws." He settled in California and died at ninety-eight. The longer he lived, the wilder his yarns became about his outlaw exploits. Hollywood believed his tales and made a movie of his life. The title of the movie should have been "The West's Most Awkward Outlaw."[1]

❧ *Four* ❧
Murder Will Out

This last chapter was, emotionally, the hardest to write, and will probably be the most difficult to read, because it is about murder. These folktales are about killings so reprehensible that they cannot be hidden. The bones of a murdered princess testify in "The Singing Breastbone." In "The Bright Sun Will Bring It to Light," a guilty conscience compels a confession.

Murder is always punished in the world of folklore. In "Mr. Fox," the brothers kill the murderous bridegroom. In "The Stoning," the wicked judge is inflicted with sores. In "The Rose Prince," even the flowers rise up to seek vengeance.

Murder is the most foul and heinous of crimes because of the finality of death. How can justice be served when no amount of punishment can restore a life taken? The folktales that follow grapple with this timeless issue.

The Bright Sun Will Bring It To Light

(Germany)

A tailor was traveling from town to town practicing his trade. For a time, he could not get work and became destitute. One day when he did not have even a penny for food, he met a merchant walking towards him on the road. The tailor dismissed God from his heart, went up to the merchant, and said, "Give me your money or I'll strike you dead."

"Spare my life!" said the merchant. "I only have eight pennies."

The tailor replied, "You've got more money than that and I am going to beat it out of you." He beat the merchant to the point of death. As the man was dying, he whispered his last words, "The bright sun will bring it to light." And then he died.

The tailor searched the dead man's pockets, but only found the eight pennies that the man had told him about. The tailor picked the body up, carried it behind a bush, and continued on his way.

After a long journey, the tailor came to a city where he found work with a master tailor who had a beautiful daughter. The tailor fell in love with her; they married, had two children, and were happy.

One morning, the tailor was sitting at a table by the window when his wife brought him coffee. He poured it into the saucer and was about to drink it when the sun shone on the coffee, casting a reflection on the wall that danced and made little rings. The tailor looked at the rings and said, "The bright sun is trying to bring it to light, but it can't."

"My dear husband!" said his wife. "What do you mean by that?"

"I can't tell you," he replied.

But she spoke sweetly, "If you love me, you must tell me." She gave him no peace; she swore she would never tell anyone the secret.

And so he told her the story; many years ago he had been traveling without food or money, when he met and killed a man. He explained to her, "The dying man said, 'The bright sun will bring it to light.' Just now the sun was trying to bring it to light. It danced on the wall and made rings. But it was not able to bring it to light."

He implored her not to tell anyone. She promised, but after he began working, she went to a neighbor and told the story in the strictest confidence. The neighbor promised not to tell a soul. But in three days, the whole town knew about the murder. The tailor was brought into court and sentenced to death.

Sources:

- Grimm, Jakob Ludwig Karl, and Wilheim Karl Grimm. "The Bright Sun Will Bring It to Light." In *Grimms' Tales for Young and Old*. Trans. Ralph Manheim. New York: Anchor Press, Doubleday, 1977. In the original tale, the tailor kills a Jew. I changed "Jew" to "merchant" to avoid anti-Semitic connotations.
- Grimm, Jakob Ludwig Karl, and Wilheim Karl Grimm. "The Bright Sun Will Bring It to Light." In *The Complete Fairy Tales of the Brothers Grimm*. Trans. Jack Zipes. New York: Bantam Books, 1987.

COMMENTS:

One of the ways that "murder will out" is by confession. This Grimms folktale reflects a reality: people talk, especially about crimes.

Some talk is simply bragging. In my city, Seattle, there are an unfortunate number of gang-related drive-by shootings and random killings. In 1994, a couple of teenagers were driving in a car and throwing eggs at houses. Occupants in an unidentified car speeded up until they were close behind the teens and fired a shotgun, killing two boys. Arrests were made because the gang members who did the shooting bragged in the neighborhood. Many cases without witnesses or leads are solved because of such bragging.

Some people talk because it is difficult to keep a secret. Storyteller Laura Simms tells a delightful tale of a king's barber who is sworn not to tell that the king has two horns. The barber, who cannot contain himself, goes to the mountains and whispers the secret into the ground. But soon the grasses are chanting, "The king of Togo Togo has two horns." In this Grimms tale, the murderer could not keep the secret, and neither could his wife or the neighbor.

Some people talk because they have guilty consciences. It is human nature that terrible deeds, eating at the heart and mind, need to be confessed. In the movie *Quiz Show*, a government investigator tells how his uncle confessed to an old undiscovered indiscretion. When asked why he confessed, the uncle replied, "It was the getting away with it that I could not stand."

The legal system recognizes this need to confess and gives limited protection for some confessions. Confessions made to priests are usually privileged; a priest cannot be made to divulge anything he hears in the confessional. The law is not as clear about confessions made to psychiatrists. Sometimes, as in the Menendez brothers' trial in the murder of their parents, psychiatrists can testify about confessions. Generally the law deems that the value of privacy and the relationship between confessor and priest or psychiatrist outweighs the value of the confession in the search for truth.

Degrees of Murder

In this Grimms folktale, the tailor is sentenced to death. Because folktales are so old, the laws found in folktales were usually governed by the "common law," or unwritten custom during the time before crime was defined by statute. Under common law, murder was defined as the unlawful killing of another human being with malice aforethought. Malice aforethought meant the intent to kill. In common law, there were no degrees of murder; the penalty was usually death.

Because this is a chapter about murder, I have included the following information about how murder is classified by modern statute. As with most complex legal conceptions and definitions, there is much misunderstanding among most people about what a murder is and how it is punished. On television news shows, I sometimes hear the man on the street calling for the death penalty for a murder, perhaps even for a drunk driving fatality. But in the United States not every death is a murder, and not every murder is punishable by death. The federal government and each state have statutes that divide murders into categories or degrees; punishment, also set by statute, varies with the degree of murder.

The following material is a general overview of the degrees of murder. They vary from state to state. I have included portions of the Revised Code of Washington State as an example of statutory language.

MURDER IN THE FIRST DEGREE

Although generalization is difficult, many statutes define these murders as first degree:

(1) Premeditated and intentional killings. There is no agreement about what constitutes premeditation. Generally, there must be some time for reflection, rather than impulse or heat of passion.

(2) Killing during specified felonies, such as rape, robbery, kidnapping.

This is sometimes called felony murder.

Examples of partial statutes from
the Washington State Criminal Code:

RCW 9A.32.020 Premeditation The premeditation required in order to support a conviction of the crime of murder in the first degree must involve more than a moment in time.

RCW 9A.32.030 Murder in the first degree A person is guilty of murder in the first degree when:

(1) With a premeditated intent to cause the death of another person, he or she causes the death of such person or a third person; or

(2) Under circumstances manifesting an extreme indifference to human life, he or she engages in conduct which creates a grave risk of death to any person, and thereby causes the death to any person; or

(3) He or she commits or attempts to commit the crime of either

(a) robbery in the first or second degree,

(b) rape in the first or second degree,

(c) burglary in the first degree,

(d) arson in the first or second degree, or

(e) kidnapping in the first or second degree.

RCW 9A.32.050 Murder in the second degree Generally, this degree of murder is intentional murder without premeditation or a murder committed during a felony that is not included in the statutory definition of murder in the first degree.

A person is guilty of murder in the second degree when:

(a) With intent to cause the death of another person but without premeditation, he causes the death of such person or a third person; or

(b) He commits or attempts to commit any felony other than those enumerated in RCW 9A.32.030(1)(c)

MANSLAUGHTER

Manslaughter is a killing without malice aforethought. Often statutes divide manslaughter into voluntary and involuntary categories. Voluntary manslaughter is a killing committed recklessly (i.e., without intention) or under extreme mental or emotional disturbance for which there is reasonable provocation (i.e., without malice aforethought). Involuntary manslaughter is an unintentional killing with criminal negligence, sometimes called negligent homicide.

RCW 9A.32.060 Manslaughter in the first degree A person is guilty of manslaughter in the first degree when he recklessly causes the death of another person.

RCW 9A.32.070 Manslaughter in the second degree A person is guilty of manslaughter in the second degree when, with criminal negligence, he causes the death of another person.

RCW 46.61.520 Vehicular homicide When a death of any person ensues within three years as a proximate result of injury proximately caused by the driving of any vehicle by any person, the driver is guilty of vehicular homicide if the driver was operating a motor vehicle:

(1) While under the influence or intoxicating liquor or any drug; or

(2) In a reckless manner; or

(3) With disregard for the safety of others.

Death Penalty: Codes and Statutes

Some states punish first degree murder with the death penalty; other states, such as Washington, use the death penalty only for first degree murder accompanied by special aggravating circumstances. In

Washington, aggravated first degree murder must be accompanied by circumstances such as:

(1) The victim was a law enforcement officer or firefighter performing official duties;

(2) The defendant was incarcerated or had escaped;

(3) The defendant paid or was paid to commit murder;

(4) The victim was a judge, juror, or attorney performing official duties;

(5) The defendant killed to conceal the crime;

(6) There was more than one victim and the murders were part of a common plan;

(7) The victim was a news reporter and the murder was committed to hinder the reporting of the crime.

In Washington, the penalty for aggravated first degree murder is life imprisonment without possibility of parole. However, the prosecuting attorney can ask for the death penalty when there is reason to believe there are not sufficient mitigating circumstances to merit leniency.

If the defendant has been found guilty of aggravated first degree murder and the prosecutor has asked for the death penalty, a special sentencing proceeding is held. The defendant may choose to have the jury or the judge decide the sentence. Both the defense and prosecutor present evidence about relevant factors, such as:

(1) Whether there is prior criminal activity, either as a juvenile or adult;

(2) Whether the defendant was under extreme mental disturbance;

(3) Whether the age of the defendant calls for leniency;

(4) Whether the defendant will pose a future danger;

(5) Whether the defendant was an accomplice and the participation was minor.

Next, the jury or judge deliberates on the question, "Having in mind the crime of which the defendant has been guilty, are you convinced beyond a reasonable doubt that there are not sufficient mitigating circumstances to merit leniency?" In order to to impose the death penalty, the jury must vote unanimously.

Condemned to the Noose

✦

(Colonial America)

Early in the 1700s, Ralph Sutherland lived in a stone house in the Catskills. He was a man of morose and violent disposition. He had a young Scot girl as a servant. She was virtually a slave and bound to work without pay until she repaid the cost of her passage. She became weary of bondage and of the tempers of her master and ran away. Sutherland set off in a raging chase. She had not gone far before he overtook her and bound her wrists and tied her to his horse's tail. She died on the homeward journey.

Sutherland was tried for her death. At trial, his neighbors testified about his ugly temper. They believed he intended to drag the girl for only a short distance, but that the punishment had gotten out of hand. Sutherland said, "I did not mean to kill the lass." He swore that the girl stumbled against the horse's legs. The horse reared, threw him out of the saddle, and dragged the servant to death on rocks. Sutherland was found guilty and sentenced to die on the scaffold.

Before the hanging, a hearing was held. Sutherland's family, who were influential members of the community, pleaded for his life. They told the judge he had always been a law-abiding citizen. Sutherland again told the court, "I did not mean to kill the lass."

The judge pondered and then spoke, "Ralph Sutherland, you have been condemned to die by hanging. But I have heard the pleas for your life. And I believe you did not intend the death. But a woman has lost her life because of your temper and I will not lift the sentence, but I will postpone it. Ralph Sutherland, you will not be hanged until you are ninety-nine years old, if you live that long. But as a constant reminder of your crime, you must wear a hangman's noose around your neck at all times. And you must show yourself to the judges every year to prove that you wear your badge of infamy. Until then, you are released on your own recognizance."

Sutherland returned home. The next time anyone saw him, he was wearing a hangman's noose, a silken cord knotted at his throat. He remained alone, seldom spoke. His rough, imperious manner departed.

After dark, his house was avoided because some said a shrieking woman passed it nightly. She was tied to the tail of a giant horse with fiery eyes and smoking nostrils. And a curious thing, somewhat like a woman, sat on his garden wall. She had lights shining from her fingertips and uttered unearthly laughter.

Every year deepened his reserve and loneliness. Some began to whisper that he might use the noose on himself. But the years sped by. A new republic was created; new laws were made; new judges sat to minister them.

On Ralph Sutherland's ninety-ninth birthday, there were none who would execute sentence. He lived another year and died in 1801. He died in his sleep. When his family found him, his throat was still encircled by the hangman's noose. Was it from habit, or was it guilt?

SOURCES:

- Skinner, Charles. *Myths & Legends of Our Own Land*, Vol. I. Philadelphia and London: J. B. Lippincott Co., 1896. Reissued Detroit: Singing Tree Press, Book Tower, 1969. I made minor language changes to make the tale easier to tell.
- Colby, C. B. "The Ghost With the Flaming Fingers." In *The World's Best "True" Ghost Stories*. New York: Sterling Publishing, 1988.

COMMENTS:

The Death Penalty: Right or Wrong?

At the time the United States Constitution was adopted, all thirteen colonies had death penalty laws. As the country grew, each state passed laws concerning the death penalty, and the state courts and the U.S. Supreme Court ruled on the legality of those laws. The death penalty was legal in thirty-eight states in 1991. Methods of execution included electrocution, hanging, firing squad, gas, and lethal injection.[1]

The Constitution does not directly address capital punishment, but two amendments refer to it indirectly:

The Fifth Amendment says, "No person shall be held to answer for a capital, or otherwise infamous crime...nor be deprived of life, liberty, or property, without due process of law...."

The Eighth Amendment reads: "Excessive bail shall not be required, nor excessive fines imposed, nor cruel and unusual punishments inflicted."

The Constitution is silent on what constitutes "cruel and unusual punishment" and on when and how the death penalty can be applied.

The United States Supreme Court, whose job it is to interpret the Constitution, has a long history of convoluted, changing, and divided opinions concerning the death penalty. In 1878, the Court, in *Wilkerson v Utah*, 99 US 130 ruled that some kinds of capital punishment were cruel and unusual; burning at the stake and beheading were forbidden. Consequently, the phrase "cruel and unusual punishment" seemed to refer to executions that prolonged the pain of dying.

The Supreme Court did not address the issue of whether any execution was cruel and unusual until *Furman v Georgia*, 408 US 238 (1972). Furman, a poor, retarded black man, unintentionally shot and killed a man during a burglary. At trial, Furman was defended by an attorney appointed for one hundred and fifty dollars; the jury was selected at

10:00 A.M., and the verdict was returned at 5:00 P.M.

The jury sentenced Furman to death under a Georgia statute that allowed the death penalty for an accidental death while committing a crime. The Georgia Supreme Court affirmed the conviction and death sentence. The case was appealed to the U.S. Supreme Court and joined with two other cases. The Court agreed to answer whether the death penalty was cruel and unusual punishment.

The Court voted five to four to overturn the conviction; all nine members wrote separate opinions. Two judges, William Brennan and Thurgood Marshall, ruled that any execution was cruel and unusual punishment and therefore unconstitutional. Three judges did not prohibit all forms of capital punishment, but said that the state statutes were unconstitutional because the juries were allowed to impose the death penalty without guidelines and limits on their discretion. The dissenting judges said that the majority of people wanted capital punishment, and the courts should not interfere with state death statutes.

In writing for the majority opinion, Justice William O. Douglas said, based on surveys and statistics, the death penalty was disproportionately applied to blacks, the poor, and other disadvantaged groups; therefore, the death penalty could only be applied if the law protected people like Furman and gave jurors specific guidelines in making their decision.

For the next four years, there were no executions. States rewrote their death penalty laws. In *Gregg v Georgia*, 428 US 153 (1976) the Court ruled seven to two that the rewritten laws were constitutional and not cruel and unusual punishment. The Georgia statute required jury guidelines:

- The trial and the sentencing hearings were to be separate, or bifurcated.
- The jury was required to hear mitigating circumstances such as the offender's youth and emotional condition at the time of the crime.

- The jury was required to find beyond a reasonable doubt and in writing that at least one of ten aggravating circumstances existed in order to impose the death penalty. Those aggravating circumstances included prior conviction for a capital offense, risk of death to more than one person in a public place, the killing of a firefighter or police officer in the performance of duty, or a generally "outrageously heinous" nature.

After *Gregg*, other states revised their capital punishment statutes to follow the Georgia statute and began executing the backlog of condemned prisoners on death row. Texas and Florida have had the greatest number of executions.[2]

The state laws and the court decisions about the death penalty are still rapidly changing. In 1986, The Court ruled in *Ford v Wainwright*, 477 US 399 (1986) that the Eighth Amendment prohibits states from executing insane criminals. However, in 1989, the Court ruled that the Eighth Amendment does not prohibit the execution of mentally retarded people. The Court members are divided as to the constitutionality of the death penalty; new members coming into the Court and old members leaving will change the future rulings.

The Debate
PRO

The majority of Americans favor the death penalty for persons convicted of murder; in 1990, 79 percent supported it.[3] In 1881, Justice Oliver Wendell Holmes said in *The Common Law*, "The first requirement of a sound body of law is that it should correspond with the actual feeling and demands of the community, whether right or wrong." Proponents say that states should follow the will of their citizens and execute criminals.

The principal argument for the death penalty is deterrence of more murders. First, others may be deterred from committing murder because of the fear of capital punishment. In *Furman v Georgia,* Justice Potter Steward said, "In part, capital punishment is an expression of society's moral outrage at particularly offensive conduct … it is essential in an ordered society that asks its citizens to rely on legal processes rather than self-help to vindicate wrongs…. We may safely assume that there are murderers, such as those who act in passion, for whom the threat of death has little or no deterrent effect. But for many others, the death penalty undoubtedly is a significant deterrent. Second, capital punishment guarantees that the murderer will not kill again." Ed Davis, ex-police chief of Los Angeles, said, "You don't shoot a rabid dog to deter other rabid dogs; you shoot him so he won't bite someone."[4]

Furthermore, the death penalty provides revenge and retribution or "just deserts." Since the earliest times, the law has been "an eye for an eye." The Bible says in Genesis 9:6, "Whoso sheddeth man's blood, by man shall his blood be shed." The philosopher Immanuel Kant said that retribution is necessary for the moral order; that the crime of murder is so reprehensible that only being put to death is adequate punishment.

CON

The opponents of the death penalty argue that reverence for all human life is the basis for a just society. If it is wrong for an individual to take another's life, it is wrong for the state to take a life. Italian jurist Cesare Beccaria said in 1764, "Is it not absurd that the laws which detest and punish homicide, in order to prevent murder, publicly commit murder themselves."

There is no statistical proof that capital punishment is a deterrent.[5] Since most murders are crimes of passion with no thought of consequences, the death penalty does not prevent the deed. Also, a life sentence without parole will prevent the murderer from murdering again.

Opponents charge that the death penalty is randomly and capriciously applied. Not all murderers are executed; only a few. Whether a person is executed depends on many factors: the jury, the judge, the ability of the prosecution and the defense, and the laws of the state. For example, not every state allows execution. Maine, Minnesota, and Wisconsin have not authorized the death penalty between 1950 and 1990. During the same period, Texas executed one hundred and forty people.[6]

Furthermore, the application of the death penalty is disproportionally applied to blacks and the poor. A white person who kills a black person is almost never put to death. In the two hundred and forty executions from 1976 to 1993, only one was of a white person who killed a black.[7] Although blacks are a minority in the United States, the number of black murderers that were executed from 1930 to 1990 was 1,686. The number of whites executed was 1,751.[8]

The Singing Breastbone

࿔

(Scotland)

Once there were two sisters who lived near the milldams of Binnorie. The King's elder daughter was being wooed by a young knight named Sir William. He gave her a pair of gloves and a ring as tokens of his true love.

But the fickle William began to notice the younger sister's sweet face and golden hair. His heart went out to the younger sister, and he no longer cared for the elder. The elder princess hated her sister and plotted against her.

One fair and clear morning, she said, "Sister, sister, dear, let us go and see our father's boats come in at the bonny millstream of Binnorie." They walked hand and hand to the river's bank. The younger sister climbed high on a rock to watch for the boats. The jealous sister came up behind and pushed the sister into the swift waters of Binnoire.

The younger princess was swept away and cried out, "O sister, sister, reach me your hand!" Her sister stood on the bank and did nothing. "Save me and you shall have half of all I have or shall have," pleaded the drowning woman.

"No, sister, I'll reach you no hand of mine. I will never touch the hand that came between me and my heart's love. And I am heir to all you own."

"O sister, sister, then reach me your glove! I promise you shall have your William again."

The cruel sister cried out, "No hand or glove of mine you'll touch. Sweet William will be mine, all mine, when you are sunk beneath the bonny Binnorie." Then she turned and went back to the castle.

The younger princess was swept down the river. The miller's daughter was drawing water from the river and saw something being swept toward the dam. She called to the miller, "Father! Close the dam. There is something coming down the river—perhaps it is a milk-white swan."

The miller ran, stopped the mill wheels, and closed the dam. They lifted the princess from the river and laid her on the bank. Fair and beautiful she looked with pearls in her golden hair. But she was dead and drowned.

A famous harper was passing by and gazed on her pale sweet face. He passed on by and traveled for many a mile, but he could not forget her face. Finally he turned and he came back to find the princess. All that was left were her bones and a lock of her golden hair.

He took her breastbone and shaped a harp from it. Then he strung it with her golden hair. The harper put the harp under his arm and traveled to the castle of the king. The king and queen were hosting a banquet. The cruel princess and Sir William were seated together at the high table, holding hands, and gazing in each other's eyes.

The harper played his old harp. He sang songs both sweet and sad. Then he took out the harp made from the breastbone of the young princess and sat it on a stone. It began to sing, soft and low. All was hushed as the harp sang:

> Oh, yonder sits my father, the king.
> Binnorie, O Binnorie;
> And yonder sits my mother, the queen,
> By the bonny milldams o'Binnorie.

The harp paused and the harper spoke, "One day I was traveling, and I saw a fair and beautiful maid with pearls in her golden hair. She was pale and drowned on the banks of the bonny Binnorie." The harper told how he had made the harp. When he finished his story, the harp began singing again, in the clear, sweet voice of the dead princess.

> *And yonder stands my William, false and true.*
> *By the bonny milldams o'Binnorie.*
> *And there sits my sister who drowned me*
> *By the bonny milldams o'Binnorie.*

When the harp had told the story, it snapped and broke and sang no more.

SOURCES:

- Hodges, Margaret. "The Haunted Harp." In *Hauntings: Ghosts and Ghouls from Around the World*. Boston, Toronto, and London: Little, Brown and Co., 1991. This story is originally from the ancient Scottish ballad "Binnorie."

- Manheim, Ralph. "The Singing Bone." In *Grimms' Tales for Young and Old*. Garden City, N. J. & New York: Doubleday, 1977. A similar tale is about a jealous man who kills his younger brother. A shepherd finds a bone from the buried brother and makes a horn. The horn sings of the murder, and the murderer is executed.

- Barash, Asher. "The Bone that Testified." In *A Golden Treasury of Jewish Tales*. New York: Dodd, Mead & Co., 1966. There are variants of this tale in which blood helps the bones testify. A bone from a dead father turns red when dipped in the blood of his rightful son.

- Patti, Raphael. "A Solomonic Judgment." In *Gates to the Old City, A Book of Jewish Legends*. Northvale, N. J.: Jason Aronson Inc., 1980. This story is the same as "The Bone that Testified" except that King

Solomon proposes the blood test.

- Booss, Claire. "Murder Will Out." In *Scandinavian Folk and Fairy Tales*. New York: Avenel Books, 1984. A priest found a skull with a knitting needle stuck through it and fastened it on top of the church porch. The congregation leaves the church without incident until an old woman walks under the skull. Three drops of blood fall on her and she confesses to murder.

- Alegria, Ricardo E. "The Chili Plant." In *The Three Wishes: A Collection of Puerto Rican Folktales*. New York: Harcourt, Brace and World, 1969. This is another variant in which a stepmother lures her stepdaughter to a hole by throwing in a chili bean, pushes in the girl, and buries her. The chili bean grows into a plant that sings to the brother. The girl is still alive when dug up.

COMMENTS:

Corpus Delicti

There is basis in fact for the folktales about bones that testify; it is difficult to destroy bones. For example, fossils made by the bones of extinct dinosaurs remain intact after millions of years. Murderers burn, bury, and chop bodies trying to dispose of evidence. But bones are unearthed or washed ashore. Bones remain and provide clues. Modern criminologists can trace the identity of a dead person by using dental records and forensic exams. The cause of death can even be determined.

Perhaps the doctrine of *corpus delicti* came into being because the human body is hard to destroy. *Corpus delicti* means "the body of the crime." The law requires that the prosecutor prove the *corpus delicti*, or that a crime has been committed.[1]

The issue of whether a corpse is necessary to prove the *corpus delicti* was changed in a sensational Boston murder trial in 1850. Dr. John Webster, a professor at Harvard College, was tried for the murder of another Harvard professor, Dr. George Sparkman. During an argument over an unpaid four hundred dollar debt, Webster killed the victim with a piece of firewood. Webster used his medical tools to dismember the body and then tried to burn it in the lab furnace. A suspicious janitor dug through a brick wall and found a few remains. Webster was put on trial; the grisly facts were put in evidence before a packed courtroom.[2]

The defense lawyers' tactic was to get a ruling from the judge that the *corpus delicti* had not been proven because no corpse had been produced; since science was still unable to identify bones, the prosecution had not proven that the remains were Dr. Sparkman. Furthermore, the prosecution had not shown the cause of death was murder. The judge ruled that the jury could decide whether circumstantial evidence could establish the existence of the crime.[3]

Some of the circumstantial evidence the jury might have considered is that the men were seen arguing, the four hundred dollar debt, Dr. Sparkman's unexplained disappearance, the locked lab, and the human bones. The jury found Webster guilty; he confessed during the appeals process and was hung.

The Rose Elf

❧

(Denmark)

In the middle of the garden grew a rosebush; it was filled with flowers, and in the most beautiful of them all lived an elf. He was so small that he could not be seen by the human eye. He had beautiful wings that stretched from his shoulders to his heels. His bedchamber was the clear and transparent pink petals of a rose. What fragrant air there was where he slept.

One day the elf flew about in the sunshine. He visited all the flowers in the garden and rode on the backs of butterflies. The sun set before he was finished with his fun. It was chilly. The dew was falling, and the evening breeze began to blow. He hurried to his rose, but it had closed for the night. He could not get in. He flew around the bush, but not one of the flowers was open.

There was an arbor at the end of the garden with latticework covered with honeysuckle. The elf flew toward the shaded nook, and hoped to sleep inside one of the flowers that looked like painted trumpets. Someone was in the arbor: a beautiful young woman and a handsome young man. "We must part," the man sighed and said, "Your brother frowns on our love and is sending me away. I am going on business far across the mountains. Farewell, my sweet."

They kissed, and the woman wept. She picked a rose. When her lips touched the rose, it opened and the elf flew inside. Through the petals, he heard the lovers saying goodbye. The man pinned the rose on his chest. His heart beat so hard that the elf could not sleep.

The young man walked through the dark forest. He was not alone, for another man was also afoot that night. It was the woman's evil brother, and in his hand he carried a long sharp knife. While the young man kissed the rose, the evil brother stabbed him to death. He cut off his head, and buried the head and body in the soft earth under a linden tree and near to a jasmine bush. "Now he is gone and will soon be forgotten," thought the evil brother.

He covered the newly dug earth with leaves and twigs and walked home through the dark night. But he was not alone as he thought, for the little elf was with him. He was inside a rolled-up, withered linden leaf that had fallen into the evil man's hair. The poor elf shook with fear and anger at the ugly deed he had witnessed.

Before sunrise, the evil man returned to his house and into his sister's bedchamber. The woman was asleep, dreaming about the man she loved on his long journey across the mountains. Her brother bent over her and laughed: the laughter of a devil. The leaf fell from his hair without his noticing it. He tiptoed out of his sister's room and went to his own, to sleep.

The rose elf rushed out of the leaf and into the sleeping sister's ear. He told her of the evil deed he had seen. To the sister it was like a dream. He described how her brother had murdered the young man she loved and buried him under a flowering linden tree; he explained where in the forest the linden tree was. Finally he remarked, "You will find a wizened linden leaf on your bed, and then you will know this is not a dream." The girl woke, and there was the leaf! Oh, how she cried! And there was no one to comfort her, no one she could tell of her misery. The window was open; the elf could have flown out to his rose in the garden, but he stayed in the room because he could not bear to leave the sister all alone. Several times the evil brother came. He joked and laughed. The poor sister did not dare show her sorrow.

As soon as night came, she sneaked out of the house and went to the forest to find the linden tree. Beneath it she dug up the corpse of the young man she loved. She cried and prayed to die soon. She wanted to take his body back to have it properly buried, but that was impossible. She held the head in her hands and kissed the cold, pale lips; she shook the earth out of his beautiful hair.

"This shall be mine forever," she said. She covered the dead body and walked home, carrying her lover's head and a branch of the jasmine bush that grew near the linden tree.

As soon as she returned, she buried the head of the young man in the largest flower pot she could find, and planted the jasmine branch above it.

"Farewell," whispered the little elf. He could no longer bear to see her sorrow and flew out into the garden to find his rose. Every morning he flew to the poor sister's window. He always found her standing by the flowerpot crying, her tears falling on the branch from the jasmine bush, and as the poor girl grew paler and paler, the jasmine bush grew greener. New leaves unfolded, and soon white flower buds appeared. Her brother chided her and said she must be crazy to stand and cry over a plant. He did not know whose bright eyes and red lips had become dust beneath the jasmine.

One day the young woman rested her head on the windowsill next to the flowerpot and fell asleep. The elf found her slumbering and crawled into her ear to tell her about the evenings in the arbor, when sweet-smelling roses were in bloom. And while she dreamed, her life ebbed out. She died and was reunited with the young man she loved.

The jasmine flowers, like great white bells, opened and spread their sweet fragrance throughout the room; that was their way of crying.

When the evil brother saw the flowering bush he took it into his own bedchamber. It was so pleasant to look at and smelled so nicely. The rose elf followed and flew from flower to flower to tell of the evil deed and the sister's suffering. And every flower grew a soul that could understand.

"We know everything," said the flowers. "Haven't we grown from the eyes and lips of the dead man?"

The elf could not understand how the flowers could be so calm. He flew to the bees and told them the story. The queen declared they would take vengeance the following morning.

But that night—the very first since the young woman's death—while the brother slept, the flowers on the jasmine bush opened. The invisible souls of the flowers flew out, every one carrying a poison spear. They gathered around his ears and told him stories to cause terrible dreams. When he screamed in fear, they stuck the deadly points of their spears into his tongue.

"Now we have avenged the dead," they cried, and flew back into their flowers.

In the morning the rose elf and the bees flew into the window to kill the brother. But he was already dead. People were standing around his bed. "The strong smell of the jasmine killed him," said one of the men.

The queen and the bees swarmed about the jasmine. The people tried to shoo them out. Finally a man picked up the plant to carry it out. A bee stung his hand and he dropped the flowerpot. It fell to the floor and broke. The white skull rolled from the black earth. Everyone knew the brother was a murderer.

The bees flew out the window. The queen hummed a song about the flower's revenge and the rose elf, who exposed the evil murder.

SOURCE:

• Andersen, Hans Christian. *Andersen's Stories and Tales*. Boston and New York: Houghton Mifflin Company, 1880. I simplified the language so the story is easier to read and tell.

Mr. Fox

&

(England)

Lady Mary was young and Lady Mary was fair. She had two brothers and more suitors than she could count on the fingers of two hands. But of them all, the most handsome and most gallant was a certain Mr. Fox, whom she met at her father's country house.

Who he was no one knew, but he was certainly brave and surely rich. Of all her suitors, Lady Mary cared for him alone. At last it was agreed that they would wed.

Mr. Fox told her of his home. He said, "It is in the forest. It is a castle." But strange to say, he did not take her to see it.

The day before the wedding, Mr. Fox went away "on business," as he put it. Lady Mary was curious about her future home and set out through the forest to find it. She kilted up her skirts and scampered along until she came to the darkest part of the forest. There she saw a castle standing all by itself with high walls and a deep moat.

She walked over the drawbridge and up to the gateway. On the arch, carved in stone, she saw these words:

BE BOLD, BE BOLD, BE BOLD

And she thought, "Well, I'm a bold one, I am." And she walked through the gate and across the wide, empty courtyard.

Lady Mary came to the big oaken doors, and on the portal was written:

BE BOLD, BE BOLD, BUT NOT TOO BOLD

She thought, "It's not too bold to enter my future home." She pushed open the big doors and went into the hall. It was as still as a tomb. A broad stairway led to a chamber above.

She climbed the stairs, and over the door of the chamber she saw:

BE BOLD, BE BOLD, BUT NOT TOO BOLD,
LEST YOUR HEART'S BLOOD SHOULD RUN COLD

Lady Mary plucked up her courage and opened the door and went into the chamber. And what do you think she saw? The bodies and bones of beautiful ladies—all broken and covered with blood.

She turned and ran from that horrid room. She ran down the stairs. When who should she see through the window? Mr. Fox—dragging a beautiful, dead woman in a white wedding dress. Lady Mary hid behind a cask on the landing.

Mr. Fox came in and dragged the woman up the stairs. On the landing, he spied a gold band on her hand and tried to pull it off. The ring was tightly fixed, so Mr. Fox drew his sword, raised it, and chopped off the hand. It flew into the air, behind the cask, and onto Lady Mary's kilted lap. Mr. Fox looked around for the ring, but did not look behind the cask. Instead he grabbed the woman by the hair and dragged her up the stairs and into the bloody chamber above.

Lady Mary ran from the castle and through the woods to her father's house.

The next morning was the wedding breakfast. Mr. Fox came to sign the marriage contract. The guests were gathered around the table in the great hall. Mr. Fox came in and sat opposite Lady Mary in her bridal array. He looked at his bride and said, "How pale you are this morning, my dear."

She sat with her eyes downcast and answered, "I had bad dreams last night."

"Tell us your dreams, my dear. And the sound of your sweet voice shall while away the hour till the time that we are wed."

"I dreamed—," said Lady Mary in a whisper, "I dreamed that yestermorn I walked through the forest in search of your home. I found it—a strong castle with high walls and a deep moat. And over the gate was written:

BE BOLD, BE BOLD

Mr. Fox replied, "Well, it is not so."

"I dreamed that I walked through that gate up to the doors of your castle, and over them were carved:

BE BOLD, BE BOLD
BUT NOT TOO BOLD"

"But it is not so and it was not so," said Mr. Fox.

"In my dream I pushed open the big doors and went into the castle and up the stairway leading to a chamber above. I saw a door, and over it was written:

BE BOLD, BE BOLD, BUT NOT TOO BOLD,
LEST YOUR HEART'S BLOOD SHOULD RUN COLD."

"But it is not so and it was not so. 'Twas but a dream—"

"In my dream, I opened the door of the chamber and what did I see within? The bodies and bones of beautiful ladies—all broken and covered with blood. And in my dream, I ran from that room and down the stairs. When who did I see? You, Mr. Fox." She looked him straight in the eye and spoke in a loud, clear voice. "You dragging a dead woman up the stairs. I hid behind the cask on the landing. When you came alongside the cask, you stopped and drew out your sword and hacked at her hand to get at a ring. The hand flew into the air and behind the cask and onto my lap."

Mr. Fox rose from his chair. His face grew pale, and as he spoke, his eyeteeth showed like a fox beset by hounds. "But it is not so and it was not so and God forbid it should ever be so."

"But it is so and it was so, and here's the hand and ring to show."

And so saying, Lady Mary rose from her chair, took the hand from her pocket, and pointed it at Mr. Fox.

Her brothers drew their swords and pulled Mr. Fox from the hall. What they did to him, I dare not tell you, lest your heart's blood should run cold.

SOURCES:

• Steel, Flora Annie. *English Fairy Tales*. New York: The MacMillian Co., 1918.

• De La Mare, Walter. *Animal Stories*. New York: Scribner's, 1939.

• Jacobs, Joseph. *English Folktales*. New York: G.P. Putnam's Sons.

• MacDonald, Margaret Read. *Twenty Tellable Tales*. New York: The H. W. Wilson Co., 1986.

• Yolen, Jane. *Favorite Folktales from Around the World*. New York: Pantheon Books, 1986.

COMMENTS:

The folktale "Mr. Fox" is about a serial killer. Serial killers have always been fascinating because there are so many unanswered questions about why they kill. Ted Bundy was a modern serial killer who, like Mr. Fox, appeared gallant, and who preyed on beautiful young women. Bundy took his secrets to the electric chair; he never revealed the number of his victims or where their bodies were located. Ted Bundy interested me because he went briefly to my law school in 1973, and I lived in

Washington when the beautiful young women began disappearing.

Ted Bundy: Serial Killer

In March 1974, a pretty student left her residence hall at Evergreen State College for a short walk to a jazz concert. She never reached the student lounge. In April, on the campus at Central Washington State, a woman left her residence hall for a meeting and disappeared. Two other women reported that a young man with an injured arm had asked them to help carry his books to his Volkswagen in a darkened area. They became frightened and fled.

The disappearances continued; a student disappeared from the campus at Oregon State University on 12 May 1974. In June, a young woman disappeared from Greek Row at the University of Washington campus; she vanished in the block between her boyfriend's fraternity house and her sorority house.[1]

The disappearances continued. On a sunny Sunday in July, two young women vanished from a crowd of 40,000 people at Lake Sammamish Park, one at 12:30 P.M. and one at 4:30 P.M. A woman in the park reported that a handsome young man with his arm in a sling had asked for help driving his Volkswagen to get his sailboat. In September, two hunters found the skulls and bones of the missing women in the woods near the lake.[2]

The disappearances in the Northwest stopped when Ted Bundy moved to Salt Lake City, Utah, to attend law school. In November, Bundy approached a pretty teenaged girl in a shopping mall and introduced himself as a police officer. After luring her to the parking lot on the pretext that her car had been burglarized, Bundy got her in his old Volkswagen. The girl escaped before he could hit her with a metal bar; she was the only living witness against Bundy. Almost immediately, he was captured and convicted of aggravated kidnapping.[3]

Bundy's arrest set off investigations by police departments throughout the West. In 1977, Bundy was extradited to Colorado to stand trial for the murder of a woman at a ski resort. He escaped, was captured, and escaped again.[4]

Two weeks later, five women were attacked while sleeping in their sorority house in Tallahassee, Florida; two died. Bundy was captured in a stolen Volkswagen and stood trial. The only direct evidence to link him with the crimes was testimony by a dentist that bite marks on one of the victims were made by Bundy. Assisting with his own defense, Bundy was so handsome and charming that young women crowded the courtroom. He was found guilty and given two death sentences.

Next, he was tried for the murder of a twelve-year-old girl who had vanished between her house and school. The verdict was guilty. On the day the jury was deliberating whether to recommend a life sentence or death, Bundy staged a surprise wedding in the courtroom. The bride was a woman who had worked with Bundy in Washington and had been corresponding with him. She was testifying on his behalf when he asked, "Will you marry me?"

"Yes," she replied.

Bundy responded, "Then I do hereby marry you." A notary was present to sign the marriage license and make the marriage valid. The jury deliberated for an hour before recommending death.[5]

In 1989, after years of appeals, Bundy was electrocuted. Crowds gathered outside the prison; the opponents of the death penalty were outnumbered by the cheering supporters who set off fireworks and held signs that said, "Welcome to the Bundy Barbecue." Bundy was suspected of killing more than thirty-five women, but he took that knowledge to the electric chair.

The Furies

&

(Ancient Greece)

At the end of the Trojan War, the triumphant warrior and king, Agamemnon, returned from Troy to Mycenae. He brought back as his slave the seeress, Cassandra. He arrived at dawn in a chariot. His wife, Clytemnestra, greeted him with spread-out purple carpets and fires kindled at the altars. But Clytemnestra had murderous intentions; before leaving, Agamemnon had sacrificed one of their daughters to get a good wind for his warships sailing to Troy. During Agamemnon's absence, his wife, Clytemnestra, took a lover, Aegisthus, and plotted murder. When Agamemnon went to the bath to prepare for his banquet of honor, Clytemnestra and her lover ensnared him in his robe and struck him three times with an ax. Then Clytemnestra sought out Cassandra and murdered her.

Clytemnestra also intended to murder her young son, Orestes, to prevent him from avenging his father's death and regaining the throne when he reached manhood. But Orestes was rescued by his sister, Electra, and sent to be raised by an uncle in another country. As Orestes grew older, he received letters from Electra saying that it was his duty to avenge his father's death.

Upon reaching manhood, Orestes sought advice from the oracle at Apollo's temple at Delphi. The priestess oracle sat on a tripod chair and contacted Apollo while in a trance. She urged Orestes to commit the murders. "Give them their turn of death, blaze like a bull upon them, to hurt and strip them bare." The oracle warned that if Orestes failed to avenge his father's murder that a terrible fate would be inflicted on him. The Furies, the spirits who punished offenders against blood kin, also called the Erinyes, would raise up from the drops of his father's blood. "They will batter and whip your carcass with a bronze-tipped scourge."

In secret, Orestes returned to his homeland. He visited his father's grave where he placed a lock of his hair as a symbol of mourning and reaching manhood. His sister, Electra, came to visit the grave, and found her brother. After hearing the plans, Electra urged Orestes to complete them.

Disguised as a traveler, Orestes went to the palace. He found his mother's lover, Aegisthus, sitting on the throne; Orestes killed him. When Orestes found his mother, she pleaded for her life. Clytemnestra said that she dreamed she gave birth to a snake, and when she cradled it to her bosom, the snake bit her and sucked out both her milk and blood. She asked Orestes, "Are you the snake I bore?" His answer was to drive a sword through her heart.

Immediately, the avenging spirits of the Furies rose up from Clytemnestra's drops of blood. The Furies were three beautiful, terrible women clad in black. Their eyes dripped blood, and their hair was tangled with serpents. They relentlessly pursued Orestes from land to land and drove him into madness.

At last, Orestes took refuge with the goddess Athena in her temple in Athens. He placed his cause before her. "Athena, my father was Agamemnon, admiral of the fleet, who was butchered by my mother. On command of Apollo, I returned from exile and cut her down. Right or wrong, you are my judge; I bow before your verdict."

Athena, goddess of war and thunder, was also wise and just. She summoned twelve of Athen's best men "to judge at this first murder trial."

Athena presided over the court and heard both sides. The Furies hissed and howled their case against Orestes, and took no consideration of his duty or divine command to kill his mother. Orestes admitted his guilt; he asked the Furies why they had not pursued his mother for her murderous deed. They answered, "Because she was not of the blood of the one she killed."

Apollo, the Sun God and son of Zeus, appeared to defend Orestes. He said that Orestes' deed was committed at the request of the great god Zeus. He pleaded that although the jury had taken an oath to give a verdict based on the evidence, they must yield to a higher principle of divine mercy.

The jury voted by dropping their ballots into an urn; bronze for acquittal and wood for condemnation. The votes were evenly divided six to six; Athena cast the vote in favor of acquitting Orestes. Athena then named the hill where they stood "Areopagus" and established the Council of Areopagus as a judicial tribunal.

The Furies railed against Athena, but she placated them. She asked them to give up their bitter missions of vengeance and become enthroned in their own shrine. And so it was that the Furies became the Eumenides or Gentle Ones.

SOURCES:

- Aeschylus. *The Orestes Plays of Aeschylus (The Agamemnon; The Libation Bearers; The Eumenides)*. Trans. Paul Roche. New York: Mentor, Penguin Books, 1962. My version of *The Oresteia* is based primarily on the plays of Aeschylus. I had to simplify the plot and number of characters to make the story short and easy to understand for those unfamiliar with Greek myths.

- Barthell, Edward E. *Gods and Goddesses of Ancient Greece* (Coral Gables, Florida: University of Miami Press, 1971.

- Gayley, Charles Mills. *The Classic Myths in English Literature and Art.* New York: Ginn and Company, Blaisdell Publishing Co., 1893.
- Green, Roger Lancelyn. *The Tale of Troy.* London: Puffin Books, 1958.
- Guerber, H. A. *The Myths of Greece and Rome.* London: George G. Harrap and Co. Ltd., 1907.

COMMENTS:

Ancient Greek Myths

In ancient Greece, the word *mythos* meant "story" or "tale."[1] Some myths explain the origins of the world and the gods on Mount Olympus, such as how Prometheus, one of the Titans, created man out of earth and water.[2] Other myths tell about epic events which are based partially on history and partially on fiction, such as the *Iliad* and the *Odyssey*. Homer's *Iliad* tells how the Mycenaean King Agamemnon sailed to Troy, besieged and destroyed the city; the *Odyssey* tells of the wanderings of Odysseus after the Trojan War.

Although the origin of Greek myths is uncertain, one current theory is that myths developed in Mycenae during the Bronze Age (1450-1100 B.C.). The first mention of the Greek gods was found on clay tablets that were used to keep the palace accounts. The tablets listed offerings of produce and gold to Zeus, Athena, and Apollo.[3] In addition, most of the heroes and cities of the Homeric epics were from the time that Mycenae ruled as a great seafaring civilization.

However, few scholars believed there was any factual basis for the Greek myths about the Trojan War until Heinrich Schliemann, a German-born amateur archaeologist, made remarkable discoveries. As a boy raised on the Homeric myths, he vowed to find the lost city of Troy. He went to Turkey in 1870, began digging, and discovered the ruins of Troy.[4] The ruins substantiated the occurrence of the Trojan War. The remains of a massive wall show that it had been built to withstand battering; storage pots dating from around 1200 B.C. suggest a long siege. Also, Mycenaean pottery, with its distinctive black stripes, was found at the site.[5]

Schliemann next resolved to prove that Agamemnon was real. In 1876, guided by ancient descriptions of Mycenae, he dug thirty-four shafts. When he discovered a royal tomb and gold mask, he mistakenly claimed they were Agamemnon's. He had actually uncovered the ruins of the great palace Homer described.[6] Remains included pottery, jewelry, and utensils made of bronze, silver, and gold, and clay tablets with a simple picture writing called Linear B.[7]

Mycenae was burned and sacked about 1200 B.C.[8] About 1100 B.C., primitive, warlike people that historians call the Dorians swept into Greece. The Dorians gained superiority partially because of their swords and weapons of iron. Greece sank into a dark time, called the Iron Age, that lasted more than four hundred years.[9] Knowledge of writing techniques, such as Linear B, was lost. The epic poems about the triumphs of Agamemnon and the Trojan War were probably passed orally from poet to poet. [10]

By 800 B.C., Greeks began to write again; some of the oral poetry was written down. The *Iliad* and the *Odyssey* were attributed to Homer. As legendary as his heroes, Homer was supposed to be a blind, wandering minstrel who sang his epic poems and played accompaniment on a harp.

During the eighth century B.C., clans and villages banded together for protection around citadels; city-states, such as Athens and Sparta, slowly developed. Although these city-states shared a common language and religion, they remained fiercely independent and never united. The city-states developed radically dissimilar political structures. The inhabitants of Sparta were primarily Dorians who developed a disciplined, military government.[11]

By contrast, Athens gradually developed from a monarchy into an aristocracy, and then into the world's first democracy. The king was replaced by a group called the archons, chosen from high-born aristocrats. After completing their terms of office, the archons became life members on the Council of Areopagus. The Council, or Senate, as it was also called, met in the cool of the evening on the hill of Areopagus. They chose and advised the archons and acted as judges.[12] It was this Council that judged Orestes in Aeschylus' play.[13]

Aeschylus and Greek Justice

With achievements in literature, sculpture, philosophy, and architecture, Greek civilization reached its Golden Age in fifth-century Athens. It was during the Golden Age that Aeschylus wrote *The Oresteia* trilogy. In 458 B.C., his plays won the prize in the contest held by the government.

The Greek dramas were usually based on the well-known myths about the gods and goddesses. They were mostly presented three times a year in Athens in outdoor amphitheaters; the theater of Dionysus seated fourteen thousand people.[14]

Aeschylus wrote about "the first murder trial" and a jury of twelve men in *The Eumenides*, the last play of his trilogy. Therefore, it is tempting to conclude that the United States jury system had its start in Athens. However, the Greek system of justice did not directly influence our system. Although there have always been differing opinions among scholars about the origins of trial by jury, the prevailing modern view is that our system had its roots in England after the Norman invasion from France.[15]

Aeschylus' *The Oresteia* is still important for the light it sheds on contemporary discussions of retribution. On one level, Aeschylus is telling the myth about the tragic House of Atreus and the hereditary curse of murder and revenge in generation after generation. On another level, he is telling about the emergence of law.[16] During the Iron Age, there were no governments or kings; families and clans were the social unit. The predominate legal concept was private delict (or private wrong) or "taking the law in one's own hands." Vengeance was a matter of family honor and right; sons had to avenge their murdered fathers or face disgrace.[17]

Fortunately during Greece's Golden Age, the endless cycles of blood feuds were stopped by legal process. In 621 B.C., a man named Dracon was commissioned to write down and codify the unwritten laws of Athens.[18] Dracon began to assert the right of the State to intervene in blood feuds; thereafter, the Council of Areopagus began trying all cases of homicide.[19] Dracon introduced the concept of intention and distinguished between intentional murder and accidental manslaughter.[20]

Pericles was the leading statesman from 461 to 429 B.C. He transferred all judicial power, except for the judging of murder cases, from the Areopagus to the people's court called the Heliaea.[21] Each year, about six thousand male citizens of Athens were selected from volunteers and divided into ten sections of five hundred or more jurors, or dicasts. Because the wage for being a juror was low, mostly the uneducated men volunteered. Trials were held in a single day with large numbers of jurors for important cases. There were no judges or attorneys; the trial resembled debates between the contending parties. The jurors voted by dropping discs into a pot; some discs were solid and some discs had holes in the centers to mean "Guilty" or "Not Guilty."[22]

Orestes' trial symbolized all these changes in the law. In the play, Athena formed a tribunal to take revenge out of the hands of the murderer and the victims. She established a trial procedure to hear evidence from both sides in a reasoned manner. Athena also invited the Furies to become part of the "new order."

Yale law professor, Paul Gerwitz addresses the importance of the Furies in his article "Aeschylus Law."[23] To Gerwitz, the Furies represent "complex forces of passion, linked at various points in the plays with vengeance, fear, anger, violence, conscience, instinct, the sense of hurt, memories of grief, the primitive, the emotional and nonrational."[24] These forces had to be channeled, honored, and included in the legal system; rational law and passionate revenge are inseparable. Gerwitz says,

> Thus, *The Oresteia* stands behind those in contemporary debate who insist that retribution must play a central role in a system of criminal justice and who warn that if retributive emotions are ignored they will be unleashed in less acceptable ways.[25]

Trial of Socrates

If Orestes was vindicated by Athenian justice, Socrates was martyred by Athenian injustice. Orestes' fictional trial was written during the democratic rule of Pericles; Socrates's historical trial was held during the dismal time after Athens was conquered by Sparta. His death marked the end of the Golden Age of Pericles.

In 399 B.C., the "wisest" Greek, Socrates, was put on trial. The trial of Socrates cannot be understood without examining the events in Athens. He was brought to trial when the city was in collapse. Decades of war with Sparta had weakened Athens. Plague, in 430 B.C., killed one-third of the people, including Pericles. In 414 and again in 406, the navy was destroyed. The state treasury was empty. When Athens surrendered to Sparta in 404 B.C., the democracy was abolished and a tyranny of the Council of Thirty established. Fifteen hundred citizens were put to death for political and personal reasons; thousands were exiled.

When democracy was reestablished in 403 B.C., Socrates criticized the election of politicians, because he thought leaders should be chosen from the intellectuals and well-educated.[26] The citizens were exhausted, broken in spirit and intolerant; it was time to silence or exile Socrates.

Socrates was tried before five hundred and one male citizens, or dicasts, in the Court of Heliaea. The indictment read, "Socrates is guilty on the grounds that he does not recognize the gods recognized by the state; he is further guilty on the grounds that he corrupts the youth." The penalty was death.[27]

Athens was small enough that all the jurymen knew Socrates. On the one hand, he had won admiration for his courage and endurance in the Peloponnesian War with Sparta, a city-state in southern Greece. Socrates was a hoplite, one of the fierce foot soldiers who fought in close formation clad in breastplate and helmet, carrying a spear and sword.[28] On the other hand, he had angered the people with his philosophy. Since his youth, Socrates had been out among the people in the markets, gymnasiums, workshops. He engaged in dialogues with anyone who was willing. He would pose a broad philosophical question, such as "What is justice?" Listening for faults in reasoning and logic, Socrates would continue asking questions until the faulty definitions and assumptions were exposed, usually in front of a crowd. He angered some people because he only asked questions and gave no answers. To many Athenians, he appeared as an intellectual snob who tore down the beliefs of the people.

Plato, the philosopher and student of Socrates, was reportedly present at the trial as a court reporter.[29] According to Plato's account of Socrates' defense speech in the *Apology*,[30] three men brought charges. Meletus, a mediocre poet, spoke first, and accused Socrates of impiety because his speculations about physical science had rejected the gods of Athens. He also accused Socrates of ridiculing the poets who were divine seers and teachers.

The second accuser was Lycon, a professional rhetorician, who knew the law. He cited the cases where impiety had been punished. Although the charge was vague and seldom used, two other prominent thinkers, Anaxagoras and Protagoras had been prosecuted for "impiety."

Anaxagoras, Socrates' first teacher, had been tried for studying astronomy and teaching that the sun was not a god, but a red-hot mass. He was condemned, but escaped and died in exile. Protagoras was the most famous of the philosophers called Sophists. The Sophists charged high fees to teach logic and rhetoric. After Protagoras wrote, "With regard to the gods I know not whether they exist, or what they are like," he was banished and his books burned. Socrates had studied with the Sophists.

The third accuser, Anytus, was a politician who was tired of Socrates' attacks on politicians. Anytus accused Socrates of corrupting the youth, by which he meant that Socrates influenced the young men to question the accepted beliefs and wisdom of their elders. In fact, the son of Anytus had been Socrates' follower and had become a drunkard. Anytus referred to other students: Alcibiades, who turned traitor and fled to Sparta during the war; Critias, who had been one of the tyrants on the Council of Thirty.

Socrates, who was seventy years old, came to court in his customary garb; a ragged robe and barefoot. In a culture that revered physical beauty, he was ugly; his body was short, his mouth large, and his nose misshapen. But his mind was still clear. The old philosopher had an opportunity to answer the charges. He refused to ask for mercy or bring his wife and three sons to plead for him. Instead, he responded in his customary way, by attacking the logic of his accusers.

He said that he had been slandered on the charge of impiety. The playwright Aristophanes had falsely portrayed him in *The Clouds* as a fool who worshiped the clouds. "I have nothing to do with physical speculations."

Socrates reminded the jurymen that when one of his students asked the oracle at Delphi, "Is anyone wiser than Socrates?" the response had been, "No one is wiser." Socrates said that he knew nothing and was superior to those who thought they knew everything. He had tried to find a man wiser than himself; he had questioned men considered wise: politicians, poets, and artisans. By exposing their pretensions, he had made enemies. He said that he had the advantage of knowing that he knew nothing. "And I am called wise, for my hearers imagine I myself possess the wisdom I find wanting in others; but the truth is, O men of Athens, that God only is wise...."

As to the charge of corrupting the youth, Socrates said he was not a teacher, never took money for teaching, and taught no doctrine. Furthermore, most of the youth who had listened to his dialogues grew up to become sensible citizens. But some young men later copied Socrates' methods to examine others. Those who were examined were angry, not with the youth, but with the philosopher.

Socrates said that God had ordered him to fulfill the philosopher's mission of searching into himself and other men. He vowed that if he were released he would continue to interrogate, examine, and cross-examine. "If you kill me, you will injure yourselves more than you will injure me. You will sin against God for killing the gift he sent you. I am a gadfly attached to the State by God, and all day long and in all places I am always fastening upon you, arousing and persuading you and reproaching you."

By a majority of sixty votes, the jury voted guilty. Meltus urged the death penalty. Socrates was expected to propose banishment, but he proposed paying a fine of thirty minae (a sum that would have been a generous dowry for a middle-class girl). By a majority of sixty-eight votes, the jury voted for death. Socrates said that to die was best; he looked forward to release from the world. "But now is the time for us to go away, I to die, you to live. Which of us is going to a better fate is unknown to all save God."

Socrates was held in prison for a month; his friends offered to arrange an escape. Socrates refused; he said that although the verdict was unjust, it was legal. He drank a cup of hemlock, as prescribed by law, and died.[30]

The Stoning

❧

(Morocco)

Once there were two brothers. One was a rich and powerful judge; the other was a poor, pious man whose greatest treasure was his wife. "A virtuous wife has a price beyond rubies," the husband always told his brother.

The poor brother left to go on a pilgrimage, as was the custom of his people. Before he departed, he went to his rich brother and asked, "Will you protect and care for my dear wife?"

"Certainly," said the judge to his brother. "Now I have my chance!" said the judge to himself, because he secretly desired his brother's wife. As soon as the husband left, the judge began to woo the wife. At first he sent her fruits and sweet tidbits that she properly accepted. Next, flowers arrived daily, and the wife began to feel uncomfortable with the attention. When trinkets and jewelry were delivered, the wife returned them. One night, the judge knocked at her door. The wife spied through a peephole and saw he was carrying a large gift. She had guessed at her brother-in-law's illicit intentions. She did not respond to the knocking.

The next night, the judge returned with an even larger gift. The wife answered the door. "Why are you doing this?" she asked. "I am your brother's wife! Leave me alone." She slammed the door in his face. He left muttering, "If you will not have me, you will have no one."

The judge began to make insinuations and suggestions about the chastity of his brother's wife. At first, the villagers rejected any notion of misbehavior on her part. Next the judge hired a series of men who were passing through the village to knock on the woman's door and ask for simple things such as a drink of water or directions to the next town. These coming and goings were observed by the neighbors. They began to say, "Where there is smoke, there is fire."

The judge began to make open accusations. In front of the whole village, he accused his sister-in-law of infidelity. His fiery words inflamed the hearts of the listeners. The villagers dragged the innocent wife into the streets and threw stones at her. They left her for dead.

Later, a traveler passed by and heard moaning from under a pile of stones. He dug through the rocks and found the woman, barely alive. The traveler took pity on her and carried her home to his own wife. The kind couple nursed the injured woman back to health and invited her to stay with them.

When the wounded wife recovered, she found she could heal the sick. She cured a neighbor's fever and gave sight back to a blind man. Word of her power spread throughout the land; people came to her for their ailments and went away healed. So the wife began a new life as a healer.

Meanwhile, the judge became gravely ill. Weeping sores spread over his body and festered painfully. No doctors could cure him. The judge tried potions and prayer, but nothing worked. Day by day he grew weaker.

The husband finally returned from his pilgrimage. He found his wife gone. He hurried to his brother. "Where is my wife?" he asked.

"She is dead, stoned to death for being unfaithful!" the judge explained.

"I do not believe you!" the husband said. The villagers came and repeated the story until the heartbroken husband accepted their words. Even though his own pain, the husband saw how ill his brother was. "Brother, what is the matter with you?" he asked.

After the judge recounted the hopelessness of his illness, the husband said, "During my pilgrimage, I heard of a great healer. I will take you to her." The judge agreed; the husband placed him on a stretcher, and they set off together. When they arrived, the healer saw that the two men were her husband and his brother. They did not recognize her because she sat behind a curtain.

"Tell me about your illness," the wife asked, disguising her voice. The judge recounted his miseries and remedies he had tried.

The wife declared, "The cause of your illness is a wrong you have committed. Confess this grave sin or you cannot be healed."

The sick man said, "I am a judge! I have committed no sin!"

"Confess your sin, or you cannot be healed," repeated the wife.

The husband pleaded, "Brother, please, confess! Otherwise you will die from your horrible illness!"

Weeping with shame and remorse, the judge told his brother, "I falsely accused your wife of being unfaithful. I urged the villagers to stone her to death. I am so sorry."

After hearing these words, the wife drew aside the curtain to reveal herself. The husband embraced her. The wife said, "If it is your wish, I will cure your brother."

The husband consented. "My brother is suffering. He has confessed and repented; I forgive him. Cure him if you can."

The wife healed the judge. He rose from his stretcher, changed in body and mind. The wife and husband returned home in great happiness.

SOURCES:

- Dwyer, D. W. "The Lapidation." In *Images and Self Images: Male and Female in Morocco*. New York: Columbia University Press, 1978.
- Chinen, Allan B. "The Stoning." In *Once Upon a Midlife*. New York: Jeremy P. Tacher, Perigee Books, 1993. Dr. Chinen based his tale on

Dwyer's "The Lapidation." Chinen, a Jungian psychiatrist, discusses the themes of suffering and healing in the context of midlife tasks.

- Noy, Dov. "The Faithful Woman." In *Moroccan Jewish Folktales*. New York: Herzl Press, 1966.

- Dawkins, Richard. "The Virtuous Wife." In *Modern Greek Folktales*. Oxford: Claredon Press, 1953. Reprinted Westport, Conn.: Greenwood Press, 1974. The slandered wife is ordered to be buried alive by her husband. After being rescued, she becomes a monk. Eventually, her husband, now blind, and the slanderer, with paralyzed hands, come to the monk, and confess. When she reveals herself, her husband is healed.

COMMENTS:

This Moroccan tale of forgiveness and healing is a suitable tale for the end of a book on justice. Sometimes the courts and legal system cannot rectify the wrongs; courts cannot restore damaged property or shattered lives. But the legal system can give a fair hearing and a final judgment, a resolution of the dispute. Then perhaps forgiveness and healing can begin. Justice is not ultimately found in the legal system, but in the human heart.

NOTES FOR LEGAL COMMENTARY

One &ea WHEN MERCY SEASONS JUSTICE

THE STOLEN SMELLS (United States)
•FRIVOLOUS LAWSUITS

1. "One Plaintiff, 700 Lawsuits: Enough, Says Judge," *Seattle Times*, 16 November 1994.

SOLOMON'S JUDGMENT (Israel)
•SOLOMON THE WISE

1. T. A. Bryant, ed., *Today's Dictionary of the Bible* (Carmel, New York: Guideposts, 1982), 587-88.

2. Bryant, 194, 510, 590.

3. Nathan Ausubel, ed. *A Treasury of Jewish Folklore* (New York: Crown Publishers, Inc. 1948), 56.

4. Ausubel, 78.

5. Geraldine McCaughrean, "The Fisherman and the Bottle." In *A Thousand and One Arabian Nights* (New York: Oxford University Press, 1982).

6. Ellen Schecter, *The Flower of Sheba* (New York: Bantam Books, 1994).

7. Bryant, 54.

OOKA AND THE WASTED WISDOM (Japan)
•IN THE MATTER OF "BABY M"

1. The judge's decision is reported at 525 A2d 1128 (NJ Super Ch 1987).

2. The decision is reported in *In the Matter of Baby M*, 537 A2d 1227 (NJ 1988).

3. Kathryn Cullen-DuPont, "In the Matter of Baby M," In *Great American Trials*, ed. Edward W. Knappman. (Detroit: Visible Ink, A New England Publishing Associates Book, 1994.)

THE FISHERMAN AND THE KING'S CHAMBERLAIN (Burma)
•LAW STUDIES

1. Maung Htin Aung and Helen G. Trager, *A Kingdom Lost for a Drop of Honey* (New York: Parents, 1968), 154.

2. Lawrence M. Friedman, *A History of American Law* (New York: A Touchstone Book by Simon & Schuster, Inc., 1973), 612-13.

THE QUALITY OF MERCY (Morocco)
•WOMEN'S RIGHTS

1. Kermit Hall, *The Oxford Companion to the Supreme Court of the United States* (New York: Oxford University Press, 1992), 328.

2. *The Bill of Rights and Beyond, 1791-1991* (Washington, D. C.: Commission on the Bicentenial of the U.S. Constitution, 1991), 72.

3. Eleanor Flexner,*Century of Struggle: The Woman's Rights Movement in the United State.* (Cambridge, Mass.: The Belknap Press of Harvard University Press, 1959), 74-7.

4. Hall, 328.

5. Kathryn Cullen-DuPont, *"U.S. v Susan B. Anthony,"* In *Great American Trials*, ed. Edward W. Knappman. (Detroit: Invisible Ink Press, 1994).

6. Hall, 329.

7. Flexner, 7.

8. David K. Boykin, *Women Who Led the Way: Eight Pioneers for Equal Rights* (New York: Thomas Y. Crowell Co., 1959), 59-61.

9. *The American Almanac: 1992-1993,* 192.

10. *The American Almanac: 1992-1993,* 174.

11. Edward S. Corwin, *The Constitution and What It Means Today* (Princeton, New Jersey: Princeton University Press, 1978), 557-59.

Two ❧ A PARLIAMENT OF ANIMALS

JUDGE COYOTE (Mexico)
•CHARACTER EVIDENCE

1. John William Strong, ed., "Character and Habit," In *McCormick on Evidence*, 4th ed. (St. Paul, Minnesota: West Publishing Co., 1992).

WHOSE FAULT WAS IT? (Malaysia)
•NEGLIGENCE AND UNFORESEEABLE PLAINTIFFS

1. *Palsgraf v Long Island* R.R., 248 NY 339, 162 NE 99 (1928).

2. The injury, which was not described in the courts decision, was a stammer which developed several days after the incident. Richard A. Posner, *Cardoza: A Study in Reputation* (Chicago and London: The University of Chicago Press, 1990), 35.

THE OTTERS AND THE FOX (India)
•AVOID LITIGATION

1. Peter Hay, *The Book of Legal Anecdotes* (New York and Oxford: Facts on File,1989), 105-6.

COYOTE AND HORNED TOAD (Navajo)
•NAVAJO PEACEMAKER'S COURT

1. Michael D. Lieder, "Navajo Dispute Resolution and Promissory Obligations: Continuity and Change in the Largest Native American Nation," 18 *American Indian L. Rev.* 1, 49 (Spring 1993).

2. Raymond Friday Locke, "The Navajos and the American Conquest," In *The Book of the Navajo*, 5th ed. (Los Angeles: Mankind Publishing Co., 1992).

3. Lieder, 5, 10; Locke, 364. Many died on the march and while imprisoned.

4. Locke, 384.

5. Lieder, 37.

6. James W. Zion, "The Navajo Peacemaker Court: Deference to the Old and Accommodation to the New," In *11 American Indian Law Review* 89, 94 (1983).

7. Daniel L. Lowery, "Developing a Tribal Common Law Jurisprudence; The Navajo Experience, 1969-1992," In *18 American Indian L.Rev.* 379, 382 (Spring 1993).

8. Chief Justice Robert Yazzie, "Life Comes From It: Navajo Justice Concepts," *24 New Mexico L. Rev.* 175, 177 (1994).

9. Zion, 90.

10. Lowery, 383.

11. Chief Justice Robert Yazzie, "Life Comes From It: Navajo Justice," In *Context* (Spring 1994), pp. 29-31.

12. Lieder, 36.

13. Zion, 103.

14. Lowery, 385.
15. Lowery, 385-86.
16. Lieder, 16. Informal mediation often works best in tribal communities or among cohesive groups with common values and history.

THE BELL OF ATRI (Italy)
•ANIMAL RIGHTS

1. Emily Stewart Leavitt and Diane Halverson, "The Evolution of Anti-Cruelty Laws in the United States," In *Animals and their Legal Rights* (Animal Welfare Institute, 1990).

2. Leavitt and Halverson, 7.

3. Janelle Rohr, ed. *Animal Rights: Opposing Viewpoints* (San Diego: Greenhaven Press, 1989). This is an excellent book on this subject. It not only looks at both sides of these issues, but is one of a series by Greenhaven Press in San Diego that teaches how to analyze and evaluate arguments.

Three ❧ SOME ARE WISE; SOME ARE OTHERWISE

A BARGAIN IS A BARGAIN (Ireland)
•THE DEVIL AND DANIEL WEBSTER

1. Stephen Vincent Benet, *The Devil and Daniel Webster* (New York: Holt, Rinehart and Winston, 1965).

GENERAL MOULTON AND THE DEVIL (Colonial America)
•SALEM WITCH TRIALS

1. Richard Dorson, "Supernatural Stories," In *Jonathan Draws the Long Bow: New England Popular Tales and Legends* (Cambridge, Mass.: Harvard University Press, 1946).

2. Brandt Aymar and Edward Sagarin, "Salem Witchcraft," In *A Pictorial History of the World's Great Trials* (New York: Bonanza Books, 1967, 1985).

3. Teddi DiCanio, "Salem Witchcraft Trials: 1692." In *Great American Trials,* ed. Edward W. Knappman (Detroit and Washington D.C.: Visible Ink, A New England Publishing Associates Book, 1994). Eventually, Sarah Goode was hanged and Sarah Osburn died in prison. Tituba escaped the gallows by her confession.

4. Aymar and Sagarin, 91-5.

5. Aymar and Sagarin, 91-5.

6. Gerald Dickler, *Man on Trial* (New York: Doubleday, 1962), 96.

7. Aymar and Sagarin, 95.

8. Dr. Alan Axelrod and Charles Phillips, "Salem Puts Accused Witches on Trial," In *What Every American Should Know About American History* (Holbrook, Mass.: Bob Adams, Inc., 1992).

9. George F. Willison, *Saints and Strangers* (New York: Time, Inc., 1945, 1965), 344-45. Using good sense and moral courage, John Howland discouraged malicious charges of witchcraft in his court. He also gave Naomi a good family story to tell hundreds of years later.

THE LAWYER'S ADVICE (Denmark)
•INSANITY DEFENSE

1. Sanford H. Kadish and Monrad G. Paulsen, "M'Naghten's Case." In *Criminal Law and Its Processes* (Boston: Little, Brown and Co., 1975).

2. Lincoln Caplan, *The Insanity Defense and the Trial of John W. Hinckley, Jr.* (Boston: David R. Godine, 1984), 19. I recommend this intelligent, accurate book for further study about the insanity defense and Hinckley's trial.

3. Colin Evans, "John Hinckley Trial: 1982," In *Great American Trials*, ed. Edward W. Knappman (Detroit: Visible Ink, A New England Publishing Associates Book, 1994).

4. Caplan, "Not So Nutty," *The New Republic*, March 30, 1992.

5. Caplan, *The New Republic*, 19-20. In spite of the public distrust of the insanity defense, many doctors and legal scholars say it is a safety valve that prevents society from punishing sick people.

A ROBBER I WILL BE (Majorca)
•JUVENILE JUSTICE

1. Harold J. Spaeth, "Juvenile Justice," In *The Oxford Companion to the Supreme Court of the United States* (New York and Oxford: Oxford University Press, 1992).

2. National Institute for Citizen Education in the Law, *Great Trials in American History* (St. Paul, Minn.: West Publishing Co.,1985), 136-38.

3. From the National Institute for Citizen Education in the Law, p. 143. Because of the decisions made in Gerald Gault's case, the juvenile system has been forever changed.

ANANSI DRINKS BOILING WATER (Jamaica)
•TRIAL BY ORDEAL

1. Harold Courlander, "Ijapa and the Hot-Water Test," In *Olode the Hunter and Other Tales from Nigeria* (New York: Harcourt, Brace and World, Inc., 1968).

2. Philip M. Sherlock and Hilary Sherlock, *Ears and Tails and Common Sense: More Stories from the Caribbean* (New York: Thomas Y. Crowell Co., 1974), VI-XII.

3. Theodor H. Gaster, *Myth, Legend, and Custom in the Old Testament* (New York: Harper and Row, 1817), 280-300. Gaster's book contains an extensive list of examples of the poison ordeal in ancient Madagascar, India, and some parts of Africa.

4. Peter Hay, "Up from the Jungle," In *The Book of Legal Anecdotes* (New York and Oxford: Facts on File, 1989).

5. Frederick G. Kempin, Jr., Historical Introduction to *Anglo-American Law in a Nutshell* (St. Paul, Minn.: West Publishing Co., 1973), 54.

SHARING CROPS (United States)
•THE SLAVE MUTINY ABOARD THE AMISTAD

1. The *Amistad* story was derived from the following sources:

   • Stephen Christianson, *"U.S. v Cinque: 1839,"* In *Great American Trials,* ed. Edward W. Knappman (Detroit: Visible Ink, New England Publishing Associates, Inc., 1994.)

   • Helen Kromer, *The Amistad Revolt, 1839: The Slave Uprising Aboard the Spanish Schooner* (New York: Franklin Watts, Inc., 1973.)

   • Deirdre Mullane, ed., "The *Amistad* Case," In *Crossing the Danger Water: Three Hundred Years of African-American Writing* (New York: Anchor Books, Doubleday and Co., Inc., 1993).

THE MONEY TREE (Apache)
• MINE SWINDLERS,THE MONEY-MAKING MACHINE

1. Atelia Clarkson and Gilbert B. Cross, *World Folktales* (New York: Charles Scribner's Sons, 1980), 284-85.

2. Margaret Schevill Link, *The Pollen Path: A Collection of Navajo Myths* (Stanford, Calif.: Stanford University Press, 1956), 37-8. Coyote usually chooses to walk the yellow trail because he is greedy and lazy.

3. Marshall Trimble, "Shady Deals," In *Old Arizona* (Phoenix, Ariz.: Golden West Publisher).

4. Carl Sifakis, *The Encyclopedia of American Crime* (New York: Facts On File, Inc., 1982), 638, 446-47.

THE THIEF WHO SLID DOWN A MOONBEAM (Turkey)
•STUPID CROOK TRICKS

1. Jay Robert Nash, *Bloodletters and Badmen* (New York: M. Evans and Co., 1973), 285-86.
   Sifakis, Carl, *The Encyclopedia of American Crime* (New York: Facts on File, Inc., 1982), 372.

Four 🙋 MURDER WILL OUT

CONDEMNED TO THE NOOSE (Colonial America)
•CAPITAL PUNISHMENT

1. Lief H. Carter, "Capital Punishment" In *The Oxford Companion to the Supreme Court of the U.S.*, ed. Kermit L. Hall (Oxford: Oxford University Press).

2. Carter, 126.

3. Richard Steins, *The Death Penalty: Is It Justice?* (New York: Twenty-first Century Books, 1993), 56.

4. Walter Isaacson, *Pro and Con* (New York: G. P. Putnam's Sons, 1983), 68.

5. Isaacson, 69; Carter, 125.

6. *The American Almanac: 1992-1993* (Austin, Texas: Reference Press, 1992), p. 200.

7. Bob Herbert, "In America; Judicial Coin Toss," *The New York Times*, 3 April 1994.

8. *The American Almanac*, 200. As Clarence Darrow, the famous trial lawyer, said, "A procession of the poor, the weak, the unfit, have gone through our jails to their deaths."

THE SINGING BREASTBONE (Scotland)
•CORPUS DELICTI

1. Charles E. Torcia, *Wharton's Criminal Law* (Rochester, New York: The Lawyers Co-Operative Publishing Co.; San Francisco: Bancroft-Whitney Co., 1978), 142. In the past, it was assumed that

producing the corpse was necessary to establish that a murder had been committed (the *corpus delicti*).

2. Jay Robert Nash, *Bloodletters and Badmen* (New York: M. Evans and Company, 1973), 596-98.

3. Stephen G. Christianson, "Dr. John Webster Trial: 1850," In *Great American Trials,* ed. Edward W. Knappman (Detroit, Washington, D.C., and London: Visible Ink, A New England Publishing Associates Book, 1994).

MR. FOX (England)
•TED BUNDY

1. Richard W. Larsen, *Bundy: the Deliberate Stranger* (New York: Pocket Books, 1980), 15-50.

2. Colin Wilson, *A Criminal History of Mankind* (New York: G. P. Putnam's Sons, 1984), 643-44.

3. Larsen, 50-52, 148.

4. Colin Evans, "Theodore Robert Bundy Trials: 1976 & 1979," In *Great American Trials,* ed. Edward W. Knappman (Detroit: Visible Ink, New England Publishing Associates, Inc., 1994).

5. Larsen, 334-35.

THE FURIES (Ancient Greece)
•THE TRIAL OF SOCRATES

1. Michael Macrone, introduction to *By Jove: Brush Up Your Mythology* (New York: Harper Collins Publishers, 1992), XII.

2. Thomas Bulfinch, *The Age of Fable* (New York: Airmont Publishing Company, 1965), 21.

3. Cyril E. Robinson, *A History of Greece* (London: Methuen Educational Ltd., 1929, 1990), 17.

4. Will Durant, *The Story of Civilization: The Life of Greece,* vol. 2 (New York: Simon and Schuster, 1939), 24-5.

5. Peter Connolly, *The Legends of Odysseus* (New York: Oxford University Press, 1988), 78.

6. Durant, 26.

7. Connolly, 12, 72, 74.

8. Connolly, 12.

9. Durant, 61-2.

10. Robinson, 27-30.

11. Robinson, 44-54.

12. Michael Grant, *The Rise of the Greeks* (New York: Charles's Scribner's Sons, 1988), 41-2; Durant, 109-11.

13. Durant, 389.

14. Aeschylus, *The Orestes Plays of Aeschylus (The Agamemnon; The Libation Bearers; The Eumenides)* trans. Paul Roche (New York: Mentor, Penguin Books, 1962), 222-23.

15. Frederick G. Kempin, Historical Introduction to *Anglo-American Law in a Nutshell,* vol. 2 (St. Paul, Minn.: West Publishing Co., 1973), 50-59. J. Kendall Few, *Trial by Jury* (Greenville, South Carolina: American Jury Trial Foundation, 1993), 8.

16. Durant, 389.

17. Neil Duxbury, *Foundations of Legal Tradition: the Case of Ancient Greece, 9 Legal Studies* (1989), 241, 247, 254.

18. Robinson, 65.

19. Durant, 112.

20. Grant, 43.

21. Robinson, 69.

22. Durant, 259-61.

23. P. Gerwitz, "Aeschylus' Law," *101 Harvard Law Review* 1043 (1988).

24. Gerwitz, 1,046.

25. Gerwitz, 1,047-8.

26. Brandt Aymar and Edward Sagarin, *Laws and Trials That Created History* (New York: Crown Publishers, Inc., 1974), 5.

27. Aymar and Sagarin, 2.

28. Charles Franklin, "Socrates," In *World-Famous Trials* (New York: Taplinger Publishing Co., 1966).

29. Robin McKown, "Socrates," In *Seven Famous Trials in History* (New York: Vanguard Press, 1963).

30. Socrates left no writings. Much of what we know of him is from his pupil Plato. Plato wrote four dialogues in which Socrates was the chief speaker:

Plato, *The Works of Plato*, trans. Benjamin Jowett (New York: The Modern Library, 1928).

•*The Euthyphro*, which discusses holiness and piety.

•*The Apology*, which is Socrate's defense, his trial.

•*Crito*, which is Socrates' answer when his friends urged him to escape from prison.

•*Phaedo*, which is the account of how Socrates drank the hemlock and died.

Selected References

Aeschylus. *The Orestes Plays of Aeschylus (The Agamemnon; The Libation Bearers; The Eumenides)*. Translated by Paul Roche. New York: Mentor, Penguin Books, 1962.

Aung, Maung Htin, and Helen G. Trager. *A Kingdom Lost for a Drop of Honey*. New York: Parents, 1968.

Ausubel, Nathan, ed. *A Treasury of Jewish Folklore*. New York: Crown Publishers, Inc., 1948.

Axelrod, Dr. Alan, and Charles Philips. "Salem Puts Accused Witches on Trial." In *What Every American Should Know About American History*. Holbrook, Mass.: Bob Adams, Inc., 1992.

Aymar, Brandt and Edward Sagarin. *Laws and Trials That Created History*. New York: Crown Publishers, Inc., 1974.

——————————. "Salem Witchcraft." In *A Pictorial History of the World's Great Trials*. New York: Bonanza Books, 1967, 1985.

Benet, Stephen Vincent. *The Devil and Daniel Webster*. New York: Holt, Rinehart, and Winston, 1965.

Boykin, David K. *Women Who Led the Way: Eight Pioneers for Equal Rights*. New York: Thomas Y. Crowell Co., 1959.

Bryant, T. A. ed. *Today's Dictionary of the Bible*. Carmel, New York: Guideposts, 1982.

Bulfinch, Thomas. *The Age of Fable*. New York: Airmont Publishing Company, 1965.

Caplan, Lincoln. "Not So Nutty." *The New Republic*. 30 March 1992.

——————————. *The Insanity Defense and the Trial of John W. Hinckley, Jr.* Boston: David R. Godine, 1984.

Carter, Lief H. *The Oxford Companion to the Supreme Court of the U.S.* Edited by Kermit L. Hall. Oxford: Oxford University Press.

Christianson, Stephen. *Great American Trials*. Edited by Edward W. Knappman. Detroit: Visible Ink, New England Publishing Associates, Inc., 1994.

Clarkson, Atelia, and Gilbert B. Cross. *World Folktales*. New York: Charles Scribner's Sons, 1980.

Connolly, Peter. *The Legends of Odysseus*. New York: Oxford University Press, 1988.

Corwin, Edward S. *The Constitution and What It Means Today*. Princeton, New Jersey:Princeton University Press, 1978.

Courlander, Harold. *Olode the Hunter and Other Tales from Nigeria*. New York: Harcourt, Brace and World, Inc.

Cullen-DuPont, Kathryn. "In the Matter of Baby M." In *Great American Trials*. Edited by Edward W. Knappman. Detroit: Visible Ink, A New England Publishing Associates Book, 1994.

_____ . "U.S. v Susan B. Anthony." In *Great American Trials*. Edited by Edward Knappman. Detroit: Invisible Ink Press, 1994.

DiCanio, Teddi. "Salem Witchcraft Trials: 1692." In *Great American Trials*. Edited by Edward W. Knappman. Detroit and Washington, D. C.: Visible Ink, A New England Publishing Associates Book, 1994.

Dickler, Gerald. *Man on Trial*. New York: Doubleday, 1962.

Dorson, Richard. "Supernatural Stories." In *Jonathan Draws the Long Bow: New England Popular Tales and Legends*. Cambridge, Mass.: Harvard University Press, 1946.

Durant, Will. *The Story of Civilization: The Life of Greece, Vol. 2*. New York: Simon and Schuster, 1939.

Duxbury, Neil. *Foundations of Legal Tradition: The Case of Ancient Greece, Nine Legal Studies*. 1989.

Evans, Colin. *Great American Trials*. Edited by Edward W. Knappman. Detroit: Visible Ink, New England Publishing Associates, Inc., 1994.

_____ ."John Hinckley Trial: 1982." In *Great American Trials*. Ed. Edward W. Knappman. Detroit: Visible Ink, A New England Publishing Associates Book, 1994.

Few, J. Kendall. *Trial by Jury*. Greenville, South Carolina: American Jury Trial Foundation, 1993.

Flexner, Eleanor. *Century of Struggle: The Woman's Rights Movement in the United States*. Cambridge, Mass.: The Belknap Press of Harvard University Press, 1959.

Franklin, Charles. *World-Famous Trials*. New York: Taplinger Publishing Co., 1966.

Friedman, Lawrence M. *A History of American Law*. New York: A Touchstone Book by Simon and Schuster, Inc., 1973.

Gaster, Theodor H. *Myth, Legend, and Custom in the Old Testament*. New York: Harper and Row, 1817.

Gerwitz, P. "Aescylus' Law." *101 Harvard Law Review* 1043, 1988.

Grant, Michael. *The Rise of the Greeks.* New York: Charles Scribner's Sons, 1988.

Hall, Kermit. *The Oxford Companion to the Supreme Court of the United States.* New York: Oxford University Press, 1992.

Hay, Peter. "Up from the Jungle." In *The Book of Legal Anecdotes.* New York and Oxford: Facts on File, 1989.

——————. *The Book of Legal Anecdotes.* New York and Oxford: Facts on File, 1989.

Herbert, Bob. "In American: Judicial Coin Toss." *The New York Times,* 3 April 1994.

Isaacson, Walter. *Pro and Con.* New York: G.P. Putnam's Sons, 1983.

Kadish, Sanford H., and Monrad G. Paulsen. "M'Naughten's Case." In *Criminal Law and Its Processes.* Boston: Little, Brown and Co., 1975.

Kempin, Jr., Frederick G. Historical Introduction to *Anglo-American Law in a Nutshell.* St. Paul, Minn.: West Publishing Co., 1973.

——————. Historical Introduction to *Anglo-American Law in a Nutshell,* Vol.2. St. Paul, Minn.: West Publishing Co., 1973.

Kromer, Helen. *The Amistad Revolt, 1839: The Slave Uprising Aboard the Spanish Schooner.* New York: Franklin Watts, Inc., 1973.

Larsen, Richard W. *Bundy: The Deliberate Stranger.* New York: Pocket Books, 1980.

Leavitt, Emily Stewart, and Diane Halverson. "The Evolution of Anti-Cruelty Laws in the United States." In *Animals and their Legal Rights.* Animal Welfare Institute, 1990.

Lieder, Michael D. "Navajo Dispute Resolution and Promisary Obligations: Continuity and Change in the Largest Native American Nation." *American Indian Law Review* 18 (Spring 1993).

Locke, Raymond Friday. "The Navajos and the American Conquest." In *The Book of the Navajo,* 5th ed. Los Angeles: Mankind Publishing Co., 1992.

Macrone, Michael. Introduction to *By Jove: Brush Up Your Mythology.* New York: Harper Collins Publishers, 1992.

McCaughrean, Geraldine. "The Fisherman and the Bottle." In *A Thousand and One Arabian Nights.* New York: Oxford University Press, 1982.

McKown, Robbin. *Seven Famous Trials in History*. New York: Vanguard Press, 1963.

Mullane, Deirdre, ed. *Crossing the Danger Water: Three Hundred Years of African-American Writing*. New York: Anchor Books, Doubleday and Co., Inc., 1993.

Nash, Jay Robert. *Bloodletters and Badmen*. New York: M. Evans and Co., 1973.

National Institute for Citizen Education in the Law. *Great Trials in American History*. St. Paul, Minnesota: West Publishing Co., 1985.

"One Plaintiff, 700 Lawsuits: Enough, Says Judge." *Seattle Times*. 16 November 1994.

Plato. *The Works of Plato*. Translated by Benjamin Jowett. New York: The Modern Library, 1928.

Posner, Richard A. *Cardozo: A Study in Reputation*. Chicago and London: The University of Chicago Press, 1990.

Robinson, Cyril E. *A History of Greece*. London: Methuer Educational Ltd., 1929, 1990.

Rohr, Janelle ed. *Animal Rights: Opposing Viewpoints*. San Diego: Greenhaven Press, 1989.

Schecter, Ellen. *The Flower of Sheba*. New York: Bantam Books, 1994.

Spaeth, Harold J. "Juvenile Justice." In *The Oxford Companion the Supreme Court of the United States*. New York and Oxford: Oxford University Press, 1992.

Schevill Link, Margaret. *The Pollen Path: A Collection of Navajo Myths*. Stanford, California: Stanford University Press, 1956.

Sherlock, Philip M., and Hilary Sherlock. *Ears and Tails and Common Sense: More Stories from the Caribbean*. New York: Thomas Y. Crowell Co., 1974.

Sifakis, Carl. *The Encyclopedia of American Crime*. New York: Facts on File, Inc., 1982.

Speath, Harold J. "Juvenile Justice." In *The Oxford Companion to the Supreme Court of the United States*. New York and Oxford: Oxford University Press, 1992.

Steins, Richard. *The Death Penalty: Is it Justice?* New York: Twenty-first Century Books, 1993.

Strong, John William, ed. "Character and Habit." In *McCormick on Evidence*, 4th ed. St. Paul, Minnesota: West Publishing Co., 1992.

The American Almanac: 1992-1993. Austin, Texas: Reference Press, 1992.

The Bill of Rights and Beyond, 1791-1991. Washington, D.C.: Commission on the Bicentenial of the U.S. Constitution, 1991.

Torcia, Charles E. *Wharton's Criminal Law.* Rochester, New York: The Lawyers Co-Operative Publishing Co.; San Francisco: Bancroft-Whitney Co., 1978.

Trimble, Marshall. *Old Arizona.* Phoenix, Arizona: Golden West Publisher.

Wilson, Colin. *A Criminal History of Mankind.* New York: G. P. Putnam's Sons, 1984.

Yazzie, Chief Justice Robert. "Life Comes From It: Navajo Justice Concepts." *New Mexico Law Review* 24 (1994).

Yazzie, Chief Justice Robert. "Life Comes From It: Navajo Justice." *Context.* (Spring 1994).

Willison, George F. *Saints and Strangers.* New York: Time, Inc., 1945, 1965.

Zion, James W. "The Navajo Peacemaker Court: Deference to the Old and Accommodation to the New." *American Indian Law Review* 11 (1983).

After receiving her law degree, SHARON CREEDEN served as a deputy criminal prosecutor in King County, Washington, for several years. Since 1983 she has been telling stories about justice at school libraries and festivals around the country, and instructing lawyers on how to be effective raconteurs in the courtroom. CREEDEN received the 1995 Aesop Prize for *Fair is Fair: World Folktales of Justice*. She resides in Seattle and Tucson.